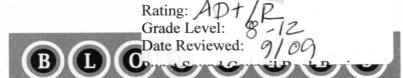

nugrl90 (Sadie)

By Cheryl Dellasega

With illustrations by Karina LaPierre

Marshall Cavendish

Marshall Cavendish Corporation
99 White Plains Road
Tarrytown, NY 10591
www.marshallcavendish.us/kids

This book is a work of fiction. Names, characters, places, and incidents are products of the author's imagination and are used fictitiously. Any resemblance to actual events or locales or persons, living or dead, is entirely coincidental.

Library of Congress Cataloging-in-Publication Data
Dellasega, Cheryl.
nugrl90 (Sadie) / by Cheryl Dellasega; with illustrations by Karina LaPierre.—1st ed.
p. cm. — (Bloggrls)
Summary: Fifteen-year-old Sadie writes on her blog about having to move to a new high school at the beginning of sophomore year due to her parents' divorce, finding and losing a true love and a best friend, and being in therapy and taking antidepressants.
ISBN 978-0-7614-5375-8 (hardcover) — ISBN 978-0-7614-5396-3 (pbk.)
[1. Interpersonal relations—Fiction. 2. Divorce—Fiction. 3. High schools—Fiction. 4. Schools—Fiction. 5. Blogs—Fiction. 6. Moving, Household—Fiction. 7. Depression, Mental—Fiction. 8. Family life—Pennsylvania—Fiction. 9. Pennsylvania—Fiction.]
I. LaPierre, Karina, ill. II. Title. III. Series.
PZ7.D3848Nug 2007
[Fic]—dc22
2007000255

The text of this book is set in Scala Sans.
Book design by Vera Soki
Editor: Marilyn Mark

Printed in China
First edition
10 9 8 7 6 5 4 3 2 1
ᴍᴄ Marshall Cavendish

To all the bloggrls in my life,
including my editor Marilyn Mark,
technical expert Chantel Piedra,
and webmistress Lory Woods

CLICKTIONARY

1: one
2: to, too (*also in* 2day, *etc*)
4: for (*as in* b4, 4ever, 4get, *etc*)
a/i: as if
altho: although
anuthr: another
awesum: awesome
b: be
BB: Buff Boy
BBF: Best Boyfriend
becuz: because
BF: Best Friend
bot: bought
brb: be right back
brite: bright
bside: beside
btr: better
btw: by the way
c: see
caf: cafeteria
cigs: cigarettes
com: come
craze: crazy
cud: could
cya: see ya
DAD: Dreadful Awful Dad
doin: doing
dyt: don't you think?
every1: everyone
fav: favorite

g/f: go figure
gonna: going to
gr8: great
grl: girl
hafta: have to
hav: have
ima: I am
imho: in my humble opinion
ITalk: give comments to Sadie's blog
kno: know
l8r: later
lik: like
LOL: Laugh Out Loud
luv: love
mebbe: maybe
mmb: make me barf
MOM: Mean Old Mom
mstm: makes sense to me
myob: mind your own business
nd: and
nemore: anymore
nite: night
ntk: need to know
nu: new
o&o: on and on *or* one and only
omg/OMG: oh my gosh/Oh My God!
oot: out of town
PDA: Public Display of Affection

pitb: pain in the butt
plz: please
pos: parent over shoulder
ppl: people
pre10ed: pretended
prinz: prince
prolly: probably
r: are
rilly: really
rite: right
rn't: aren't
sed: said
sez: says
shud: should
sic: sick
site: sight
sk8: skate
skool: school
sorta: sort of
sum: some (*as in* sumday, sumone, sumtimes, *etc*)
sumthin: something
tafw: too awful for words
tcfw: too cute for words
T-Day: Thanksgiving
tefw: too excited for words *or* too embarrassing for words
tffw: too funny for words
tgfw: too gross for words
tho: though

thot: thought
thru: through
tmi: too much information
tolly: totally
tri: try
tru: true
tuff: tough
u: you
u r: you are
ur: your
URock: # of props readers give Sadie's blog
VBF: Very Best Friend
vid: video
w/e: whatever
W3TP: What's Wrong With This Picture?
w8: wait
WS: Wicked Sister
wud: would
wut: what
wuwt: what's up with that?
wuz: was
x: *substitute for* ex– (*as in* xactly, xcept, xcuse, xtra, xtreme, *etc*)
y: why
ya: you
ykw: you know who
z: *substitute for* s (*as in*, boyz, thoz, toyz, *etc*)

My Profile
Name: Sadie
Birthday: 3/29/you guess
Gender: Female

Interests & Expertise
Interests: Reading, hanging out with friends, babysitting
Expertise: Working on developing one—shape-shifter?
Occupation: Student, sister, daughter, niece, friend

My Buddy List
nugrl90: that would be me (Sadie)
sk8r4life: my loser ex-boyfriend, Dustin
ems89: Emma, the VBF a girl could have
gr82bgoth: my big sis's BBF
nujules4u: Jules, in the same situation as me—new
kool2Bmia: Mia, also new like Jules and me
milhidi: "Mile-Hi Di," a tall girl from my old school
gr82h8sO: Ronzo, best friend of my new BBF
uduntknome: ex-girlfriend of my new BBF

Party Pals
rckzsohrd: guy
2muchfun: Emma's brother
babe4u: girl

Random Posters
hshoney90
4thelswhodied
imogaynsoru
gld4grlz
colegstud84
dmngudguy88

Chapter One

Tuesday, August 10

My wicked sister Lola's favorite saying is: "Life sucks, and then you die"—exactly what you'd expect from someone who's made it her mission to be Miss Goth USA. One time, I pointed out that this was not exactly helpful advice and that <u>some</u> older sisters support their younger sisters. Her answer?

"I <u>am</u> being helpful. You take things way too seriously. Get over yourself." (This from a girl who that very morning became hysterical when she couldn't find her black fishnet stockings with the medium squares, not the teeny-tiny ones or the way-big ones.)

You'd think my MOM (Mean Old Mom) would be upset to see her daughter looking like my WS (Wicked Sister) does, but not so.

"Lola is just trying to express herself," MOM told me one time, "and that's okay because she gets straight A's in school, volunteers at the Food Bank, and works weekends at the hospital. She also cleans her room without being asked." MOM's a therapist, so she knows better than to say, "And you don't, Sadie!" but I know that's what she was thinking.

Last year I did get an award—sort of—for *Most Visits to the School Nurse's Office.* I think I was there at least 36 times, usually because I really was sick, but sometimes I just needed a peaceful place to rest, which is, of course, impossible in school. (Even though lots of kids can sleep at their desks, they're too hard for me.) The school nurse's office is really nice—it has comfy pillows, a stereo with headphones, and cheerful posters that have nothing to do with school.

At first, Ms. Armstrong, the nurse, always gave me a cold wash-cloth for my headaches and let me lie down for as long as I wanted, but by January, I think she got tired of seeing me. She called MOM and DAD (Dreadful Awful Dad) and asked if everything was okay at home. They said we were working through some *rough spots,* which was so not true. The two of them were fighting all the time—usually so loud WS and I could hear them screaming back and forth about a divorce, even with our bedroom doors closed.

After that, Ms. Armstrong still let me come in whenever I wanted, but she gave me this lame pink book with flowers on the cover and said, "You know, Sadie, sometimes girls find it very helpful to express their feelings by writing them down in a journal. As a matter of fact, I still have the diary I kept when I was your age." a/i!

I did get an A in English last year (C's in everything else), mostly because this too-cute student-teacher guy worked with me on my creative writing. He said I had *talent,* but WS says he tells all the losers that so they won't give up and flunk out. He suggested I keep practicing over the summer and take advanced English next year, a class he just happens to student teach as well. I'm not sure blogging counts as practice, but that's how I convinced MOM and DAD to let me move the computer into my bedroom.

So here it goes—my first ever website! (Not counting the lame webpage I made when I was ten and a Smurf addict.) My VBF Emma sent me these awesome backgrounds, and note: there's no blue and no cartoons. (Although I kinda miss those little fellas.) Please give me lots of props (URocks) and comments (ITalks) so my feelings won't be hurt.

Why now, you might wonder? What has led this blog-resistant all-American girl to believe she has anything worth writing about?

Well . . . picture yourself post-traumatic breakup with your first BBF, hoping for a decent summer. Instead, you end up babysitting 2-year-old twins every single day, minus one week of vacation in July and on weekends. Everyone else is hanging out at the pool or the mall while you're chasing a pair of little boys who are both incredibly cute and incredibly bad.

You are stuck in their messy house, and it's important to note: it's their house, not yours, so why should you be expected to clean it and babysit too? (Because, in the words of DAD, the polished lawyer that he is, "Sometimes we all have to suck it up, Sadie.") I could have made more at McDonald's, but then I wouldn't have scored parental brownie points. (The twins just happen to belong to DAD's boss.)

This has been my summer: saving up some cash, sleeping over

with my VBF on Fridays, and preparing for the groove of tenth grade. The teen equivalent of happy, right?

Wrong.

One morning last week I wake up, and before breakfast I find out that:

A. My parents are really, truly getting divorced, just like they threatened to a hundred times before

B. My DAD is not only moving out of the house, he's moving halfway across the country

C. I am also moving since MOM wants to be close to her sister and get *emotional support*

D. <u>Every last one of my freakin' friends will be gone from my life forever</u>—no matter how sincerely MOM promises she will drive me back every weekend to visit since it's only 30 miles away (Last year she promised to buy me a dog for Christmas and I'm still waiting. . . .)

E. I will be starting a brand-new school in LESS THAN A MONTH!!!

Naturally, I immediately called Emma, and we cried over the phone, but then she told me she had to go shopping with some of our other BFs and hung up. I sat there looking at the phone and wondering if she really cared at all.

WS seems perfectly fine with starting her senior year in a brand-new school, but she doesn't have friends to leave anyway, just her creepy BBF Slap, whose real name is Mark. Here's his story: When he was in ninth grade, he wore a black shirt that said "I don't give a slap" for three months straight. (This was when a lot of kids were wearing shirts that had substitute words for swear words, like "fork" for f*** and all that.) No one ever figured out whether Slap had a zillion of these T-shirts or just recycled the same one over and over, but the nickname stuck.

W3TP: Half of all marriages end in divorce, but marriage vows still say "until death do us part." Isn't that asking for trouble?
Posted 8/10 at 6:30 PM

8 URock 2 ITalk

Yo, u r rite, so many kidz go thru divorce, as u kno, it happened 2 me 2. Thatz when I discovered sk8ing nd a nu purpose 4 my life.
Posted 8/10 at 8:26 PM by sk8r4life

Dustin, wut's happened is rilly bad, u shud understand Sades is sad. everybody has a pity party when something like this happens. Sadie: eat ice cream, eat ice cream, eat ice cream! (remember sixth grade nd the vanilla nut fudge bingefest, OMG it was 2 fun!) And btw, I do 2 care about you! u r my VBF since 4ever nd now I have 2 find someone else 2 eat lunch with nd hang out with at skool. We need 2 have a big get2gether (think sleepover) b4 you go! Hope u r okay, sweet one!
Posted 8/10 at 10:12 PM by ems89

Saturday, August 14
So here's how it goes: Friday the 13th was unlucky for me—we had to do so many things to get ready to move that MOM forgot people need a little downtime during their day. That meant I got a super headache and about two hours of sleep because I had to pretty much be her slave all day. That didn't stop MOM from waking me at 8 AM.

"Time to pitch in and help pack," she said, like it was a big happy family project.

When I went downstairs to get a bowl of Frooty Loops (which are not as good as the original, no matter what anyone says), all I could think about was DAD having breakfast with me, just the two of us, like he's done every Saturday for as long as I can remember. Since he's staying at a hotel until he leaves for St. Louis, I put the bowl away and had a glass of orange juice instead.

I called up Emma, but before we could make any plans, MOM (who has been in nonstop crying mode) yelled at me to PLEASE HELP OUT. I randomly threw all of my clothes and books and CDs and other stuff in boxes and taped them shut. (WS, the neat freak, has her boxes labeled and stacked in order of size.) The hardest part was taking down my pictures, because it made me remember the fun times I've had with my VBF and my BFs.

MOM should be happy. Almost everything I own is boxed away.

After I packed, I lay on my bed, staring at the ceiling, looking at those night-glow stars DAD put up when I was afraid of the dark in fourth grade. They look nice at night, but listening to MOM and WS talk about our new house, I noticed the stars were all cruddy and peeling at the edges.

My BFs have been calling and telling me they can't believe I'm moving and how upset they are and how much they will miss me and how much it sucks to have your parents jerk you around like this. Yesterday, MOM told WS that the reason they finally decided to split up is that DAD has a girlfriend he's been seeing during all the *business* trips he says he has to take.

Who meets someone on a trip and then moves across the country to be with her? I guess when he told me last week that he and MOM were going to try to work things out, it was about as true as his saying I will always be his *special girl,* right before he walked out the door. mmb.

Life is too random. You think you're doing okay despite having a *challenging* ninth grade and a traumatic breakup with your BBF, but then, for no reason, everything changes, and you're moving to nowheresville and will probably never see your VBF again, and your life is ruined forever.

W3TP: You fight a lot. You hate each other. You decide to split up. Why aren't you happy about it?
Posted 8/14 at 2 AM

2 URock o ITalk

Wednesday, August 18

Today, WS drove me to check out our new school after we dropped off a load of moving stuff. The mascot is a chipmunk, and the school colors are maroon and white—so there you have it. It's so not me. WS seems almost happy to see me sad, but that's her personality—the world is all about her. Since she can drive, she'll still get to see her beloved Slap as much as she wants, and her extreme goth world will carry on.

Our new house—or rather half a house—isn't much better than the crappy school. The bathroom has this gross shower/tub that looks like it's from the 1900s, and when MOM opened the refrigerator, we nearly puked from the smell. Just being there made my head get all funny like it does preheadache, <u>especially</u> when I found out I have to share a room with WS now. Joy of joys.

WS immediately put her creepy gothic posters all over the walls and then dared me to even touch them, let alone move them. tafw.

<u>W3TP: Waking up every morning to a six-foot poster of Fear Cult.</u>
Posted 8/18 at 3 PM

---

4 URock 3 ITalk

U need to read about wut doezn't kill u makez u braver & stronger. U could also tri the martial artz, they give happiness.
Posted 8/18 at 6 PM by sk8r4life

Super Sades—Ima gonna miss u, 4 sure, but we will be friends 4evermore. we r superslick superchicks—remember? we still hafta save the world, girlfriend!
Posted 8/18 at 9 PM by ems89

Fear Cult is THE band. Matt Riser rocks—get used to it!
Posted 8/18 at 11:05 PM by gr82bgoth

Thursday, August 19

Before you think Emma and me are conceited—the superchick thing started in second grade when we discovered there weren't any girl superheroes we liked—so we made up our own. FYI, sk8r4life, the obnoxious poster, was my first and now ex-BBF. I've known him as long as I've known Emma, but we didn't really like each other until last year.

One day at school, I happened to be walking by him and his skater crowd when I sort of tripped on this crack in the floor and fell down right in front of him. Instead of laughing like everyone else, he helped me pick my stuff up. It was the first time I really noticed him in a boyfriend kind of way.

After that, I convinced Emma to hang out at the skaters' park with me, since Dustin is there every afternoon, training for the X games. Somehow, he got the idea that I brought him good luck, and from that moment on, he insisted I had to be within sight whenever he was on his skateboard.

Almost every day after school, I went to the skate park unless it was raining or too cold. Sometimes Emma came too, but mostly it was just me, watching him practice xtreme skateboarding and thinking at any moment he would need an ambulance.

Then came the moment when he realized how bored I might be sitting there and said, "Sadie, why don't you try skateboarding?"

Of course he forgot to tell me how to stand on the skateboard without crashing instantly, and I ended up in the ER with a broken right arm. MOM and DAD got mad at Dustin because I hurt myself and had to miss school, and then when I wasn't available to worship his every move, it was good-bye, Sadie, hello any other adoring female available.

There's more, though. One day this summer when I was in the middle of scrubbing peanut butter off little faces, Emma came over all upset and told me Dustin had a complete wipeout on his skateboard and was being rushed to the hospital unconscious. I felt so bad that as soon as the twins' parents came home, I went to the grocery store and got some really nice flowers—because in science class we learned the sense of smell is very important for the brain. I made WS drive me to the hospital and had to stop myself from crying the whole way there.

I arrived at the ICU to find him wide awake with three other girls around him, sobbing and kissing his hand and saying they hoped he wouldn't die. So I threw the flowers in the trash can and left. Emma said it was just as well because after he got out of the hospital, he wasn't the same person anymore. I wouldn't know since we haven't had any real contact since then.

Anyway, Emma, I'm sorry we didn't get to spend a lot of time together before I moved. You will always be my VBF!

W3TP: A girl (my sweet sis) who makes her goth boyfriend post for her becuz she has "better things to do than zone out in front of a computer."
Posted 8/19 at 9:30 PM

4 URock 1 ITalk

itz tru, I had wut they call a *near-death experience* nd that led me 2 the Lord. U can read all about it on my blog.
Posted 8/19 at 9:45 PM by sk8r4life

Chapter Two

Friday, August 20

DAD was the last one to leave our old house today. He went to pick up a couple of things and then took a taxi to the airport all by himself and flew out of our lives.

Who moves to St. Louis, anyway? I looked it up on the Internet, and other than a baseball team he doesn't even like, their big claim to fame seems to be a West Nile Virus Information Center.

He says he'll see us all the time, but I know he won't. It's one thing to take Saturday afternoons off from your busy job and go to a movie with your daughter, but flying to Pennsylvania from St. Louis every week is about as likely to happen as me getting back together with Dustin.

Now the whole issue of money (who has it and who doesn't) has got MOM and DAD in another screamfest. MOM's going back to work so we'll be able to *make ends meet,* but a hundred times a day I have to hear about what slime DAD is because we had to sell our old house during a slow season in the real-estate market. (It's slow because other parents actually care about not moving their kids right before the beginning of school.) w/e.

It's weird having MOM going back to work after years of staying home to take care of us. She used to drive us to school and me to piano lessons on Wednesdays, but I guess music is now a thing of the past—not that I liked practicing that much anyway.

WS is thrilled since she got DAD's old car, even though it's on the condition that she has to graciously drive me to and from school every day. WS in a car is even scarier than WS sleeping in a bed three feet away.

Okay. Emma sent me this quiz to cheer me up. It's her fault I've gotten obsessed! Superslick Superchick—help me!

THREE ABOUT YOU:
NICKNAMES
1. Bunnykins (when I was 5, and from my DAD only)
2. Suck-up (courtesy of WS)
3. Superslick Superchick (only with Emma)
SCREEN NAMES
1. nugrl90
2. lovzmyvbf
3. givupthemoney
GOOD QUALITIES
1. sense of humor
2. my hair (on a good day)
3. I figured this list out
BAD QUALITIES
1. my butt

2. my thighs

3. my outlook on life (justifiably so, imho)

FEARS

1. The very middle of night

2. My sister in a bad mood

3. My sister in a good mood

TO DO'S

1. Take a plane trip by myself (I guess now I'll have to, if I ever want to see my DAD)

2. Make lots of friends instead of 1 VBF

3. Get along with MOM and WS

RELATIONSHIP DESIRES

1. A person who will tell me when I have mustard on my chin

2. Someone who will go see a movie I like, even if he doesn't want to

3. Loyalty

TWO TRUTHS AND ONE LIE

1. I love my life

2. My favorite book is *Little Women*

3. I can run a mile in six minutes

CAN'T DO'S

1. Get along with my sister

2. Eat hot dogs without a roll

3. Swim backstroke

LOVE TO DO'S

1. Torment WS

2. Add to my paper-clip collection

3. Eat a whole bag of chocolate kisses

FUTURE JOBS

1. Therapist (not surprising, given the fact that I live with a gothic maniac and my MOM's a therapist)

2. Writer

3. Olympic runner (have to get the running part down, first)

GOALS FOR YOURSELF BEFORE YOU TURN THIRTY

1. Ride a motorcycle

2. Learn how to skydive

3. Find my true love

W3TP: Long quizzes no one cares about—everywhere.
Posted 8/20 at 8:30 PM

8 URock 3 ITalk

U r hot. Plz com back 2 me. I miss u every day.
Posted 8/20 at 11 PM by sk8r4life

Superchick—don't believe a word of it. He can't w8 2 give u sh**
i heard he's going out this very nite—let's go surprise him—wut
a site! He he.
Posted 8/21 at 12:03 AM by ems89

Emma—rhyming is <u>not</u> a super power, i have nothing 2 hide, come
2 the movies 2nite if u want, I'll b there with a <u>bunch</u> of kidz.
Sades, i liked reading about u on the quiz (c—even I can rhyme.)
Posted 8/21 at 12:15 AM by sk8r4life

Sunday, August 22

OMG, yesterday was a day to die for. Me and the rest of our gang
(Meg, Lissa, Wend, and Gi) all slept over at Emma's, and it was
so fun but so sad at the same time. We started out throwing
water balloons at each other—<u>so</u> elementary school, I know, but
it was hot and we didn't want to go to the pool. Then we got

pizza and watched the whole Chucky movie series and talked about the first time we watched them in, like, second grade when we were young and innocent (yeah, right!). After that, we went online and tried to find some guys to IM, but it was kind of a slow night because everyone must have been out enjoying the last days of freedom before school starts.

We took bunches of pictures, and then Gi started crying and saying how much she was going to miss me, and Wend started crying because she doesn't have any classes with her friends, and the next thing you know, it was one big sobfest. Two boxes of Kleenex later, we swore we would always be VBFs and that in ten years we would have a reunion in Aruba.

Then, of course, we raided the kitchen and ate ice cream like there was no tomorrow. Emma had stocked up, so we each got our own container, but we shared too. I was determined to stay awake and cherish every last minute with them, but I fell asleep sitting up at 4 AM. . . .

W3TP: Crazy people get pills instead of ice cream.
Posted 8/22 at 5:54 PM

10 URock 0 ITalk

Tuesday, August 24

Tonight I went outside after everyone was asleep (everyone being MOM and WS) and laid down on our new lawn and just stared up into the sky. There were a billion stars I'm sure, and I could see them all, some real sharp like pencil points and others like a smudge in the background. For just a second, I thought maybe things might turn out okay. Maybe:

I will ADORE my new school

I will be EXTREMELY popular

I will meet my TRUE love

We will become a happy, wonderful FAMILY again and ride off into the sunset . . . or somewhere

God will make SENSE

(The God thing. Do you ever wonder when you're all alone and it's sort of creepy silent, if you're really not all alone?)

W3TP: MOM's belief: "You must go to church to keep a good relationship with God." Like it really worked for her and DAD.
Posted 8/24 at 11:15 AM

o URock o ITalk

Chapter Three

Wednesday, August 25

Finally online at new house (high priority). Computer in new (shared) room (low priority). WS being a pitb in a way only she can be. (Please, let me discover she was adopted at birth and really isn't my sister after all.) Email and phone call from DAD to say he misses me *so much* and is thinking of coming back for a visit next week. (I'm not putting any money on that one. . . .)

Am I bored or what? I found this on Emma's website—it's soooo lame. It's called:

Get 2 Kno U

Check if you have ever . . .

( ) *Given yourself a mani & pedi in the same day?* No, but Emma and I used to do each other's toes every week when we had sleepovers—with glitter and paste-ons.

( ) *Had a party that got crashed?* Just a small one on the last day of school, and my WS was the crasher.

(   ) *Spent the night with a friend?* As often as possible. Must escape WS whenever, wherever, however.

(   ) *Been naked with a member of the opposite sex?* Yeah, my DAD walked in on me by accident when I was in the shower. tefw.

(   ) *Laughed until your stomach hurt?* No, but I did laugh until soda squirted out my nose. Gross!

(   ) *Gone on a vacation that you wish you hadn't?* Oh yeah—I'm living it right now!

(   ) *Gone to summer camp?* OMG—nonstop until seventh grade.

(   ) *Swam until your skin got wrinkled?* Almost every day with my gal pals until this summer.

(   ) *Walked out of a movie?* Are you kidding? Waste all that money? There's always popcorn if the story sucks.

(   ) *Gone shopping for an entire day?* No, it's against my religion. (Just kidding—it *is* my religion.)

(   ) Gotten so bored you could cry? You got it. Right now.

W3TP: People post stuff on the Internet that they would never ever tell someone in person, even their BFs.
Posted 8/25 at 5 PM

6 URock 3 ITalk

Sadie, this is so not cool—friends r supposed 2 follow this rule: <u>never</u> make fun of a VBF, especially online—she shud b special unto death!
Posted 8/25 at 6 PM by ems89

OMG, I'm so sorry. I didn't mean <u>you</u> are lame becuz, of course, you aren't. I meant whoever invented the quiz was lame—*abject apologies* nd sound of Sadie begging forgiveness.
Posted 8/25 at 7:03 PM by nugrl90

Itz ok, I feel the same way. Just needed some stuff 2 post and that quiz interested me the most.
Posted 8/25 at 8 PM by ems89

Sunday, September 5

It's amazing how quickly you can be in a completely different life. In three days I will walk into a school where I don't know anyone, and try to survive the awfulness of a new year.

DAD keeps calling, and since WS refuses to talk to him, that leaves me to tell him how traumatic it is to wake up and see evil creatures staring down at me from all sides, courtesy of WS. When he tries to cheer me up and tells me I'll be happy once school starts, I get mad and say this is all his fault. Even if he doesn't love MOM anymore, he doesn't have to make <u>me</u> suffer too.

That usually ends the conversation, which totally sucks and gives me a huge headache. I haven't gotten up the courage to give him grief about the new girlfriend he *forgot* to tell me about, but if he gives me any more of the *I'll <u>always</u> love you, Bunnykins* crap, I will. As predicted, he's already changed his mind about coming for a visit soon.

This morning, MOM made me go to our new church and sit right up front next to her. a/i! I would be embarrassed beyond belief to drag my daughter into a place of God if I were getting a divorce, which is a mortal sin btw.

Of course, WS had a million excuses for not coming with us:

She had a headache.

She had cramps.

Sweet Slap was going to call, and she couldn't bear to miss him.

o&o it went until MOM just gave up and promised to take me out for chocolate-chip pancakes if I'd go without a fuss. The only good thing was checking out the other kids my age who were probably forced to come too. I saw two guys and a girl with potential, but in reality, I'm sure I'll end up in homeroom with the dorkfest guy who gave me the Sign of Peace.

<u>W3TP: Letting your goth daughter stay home from mass, but insisting that your perfectly normal daughter go.</u>
Posted 9/5 at 1 PM

8 URock 5 ITalk

U know, u shud b careful wut u say about God, Sades. Maybe ur life wud look happier if u turned 2 the Lord like I did.
Posted 9/5 at 3 PM by sk8r4life

Superchick girlfriend, I feel so blue! It's sad 2 think of going 2 school tomorrow without u! remember last year when u tripped in the caf nd spilled spaghetti all over our worst enemy, Mile-Hi Di? What a sign of things 2 come! (Did u kno she is moving in on Dustin?) Speaking of Dustin—what gives with the Jesus talk? He is so different from when u 2 were 2gether.
Posted 9/5 at 6 PM by ems89

u r rite, i have changed nd repented. My church is awesome with really good music, so i'm saved nd proud of it. U wud b 2 if sumthin happened 2 u like it did 2 me. When I wuz knocked out it wuz like I went 2 heaven nd saw God nd knew there wuz a reason 4 me 2 come back 2 earth—2 spread the GOOD NEWS! Already I got sum guyz 2 come 2 church with me.
Posted 9/5 at 9:20 PM by sk8r4life

u r creeping me out 4 SURE. Please don't post nemore! Things like that just don't happen 2 kids unless itz on TV.
Posted 9/5 at 10 PM by ems89

Believe wut u want—or not.
Posted 9/5 at 10:15 PM by sk8r4life

Monday, September 6

DAD called to wish me good luck tomorrow. Then tears came, and I had to hand over the phone because I was just too sad to talk to him. MOM started yelling at him, but then after they hung up, she came over to the sofa and tucked me up against her and we both cried. After about five minutes, she stopped and said she was going to make me some popcorn with extra butter, my personal favorite snack, and sent WS to the store to get us a video. "Something funny!" she said, so WS came back with *Life is Beautiful*. She told MOM, "It has humor!"

Don't watch this movie if you are in even a remotely sad mood.

W3TP: Dads in St. Louis and daughters in Pennsylvania?
Posted 9/6 at 9 PM

2 URock 1 ITalk

U r rite about ur sister, she is just wrong, b glad u won't have 2 live with her long! (Remember the time she turned all her white stuffed animals in2 goths using black magic marker?) But hang in there nd things r sure 2 get better. u kno ur dad is crazy about u nd will come visit soon.
Posted 9/6 at 11 PM by ems89

Tuesday, September 7

NuGrl at School: A Quiz
Are You a Leader or a Loser?
1. You discover on the first day of school that "cliques" are already in place. You:

    A. Give up on the year because you don't have a group

    B. Try to worm your way into a group

    C. Create your own group of kids who aren't in any other group

2. You go to the cafeteria and discover there is no place for you to sit. You:

    A. Throw your lunch in the trash and go sit in the library until lunch is over

B. Squeeze yourself into a space at an already full table

C. Make a sign that says "New Kids Welcome" and start a table of your own

3. In English class, the teacher gives a group assignment. Obviously, you don't know anyone in class. You:

A. Beg the teacher to change the group assignment to an individual one

B. Demand that the girl in front of you let you in her group

C. Stand up and graciously announce that you are available for inclusion in a group

4. You wear a shirt that was fine in your old school but is clearly out of style in your new school. Everyone says it looks like a parachute. You:

A. Dissolve into tears and run to the school nurse's office

B. Make fun of the tight short shirts they're all wearing

C. Cleverly knot the bottom of your shirt so it becomes not only formfitting but fashionable

5. At your locker, a cute boy asks if you could try his lock, as he can't seem to get it open. You:

A. Suspect it is a setup and tell him no

B. Mumble that you probably wouldn't be any better at opening it than he is

C. Say, "Sure," and open the locker for him

These are all things that happened to me on my first day of school, and while I would like to say that I made the "C" (i.e. leader) choices, I did not. However, Jules, another new girl I met, did. She invited me into her group, drew this funny sign for our table at lunch, got both of us *invited* to work with two buff guys on the English assignment, AND she fixed my shirt. The last thing (#5) really happened, but before I could do A, B, or C, the guy yanked on the handle one last time and it popped open. End of conversation. Sigh.

Jules is in all my classes, but you'd never know she was new too. When she walked into homeroom, instead of scurrying to her seat like a little mouse (as yours truly did), she paused—yes, paused—for a second in the doorway, looked the room over, and smiled to herself. Then she sat down.

Okay, I'm back to believing there might be a God and that Jules is my own personal angel. She's from New York City, which is too cool, and wears these vintage-looking clothes I've never seen before, AND her dad is some kind of celebrity. Her parents sent her here to live with her older sister because she was having a few problems (her words) in the city. w/e—I'm just relieved to have someone nice in all my classes, and I hope she'll still hang around with me tomorrow.

W3TP: When adults move they *relocate,* but when kids move they get labeled as *the new girl* or *the new boy* for an entire year. Isn't everyone new in some way on the first day of school? *Posted 9/7 at 4 PM*

6 URock 2 ITalk

Glad 2 hear u had a good day nd that things r going ur way. U wouldn't believe how much things have changed here nd how lucky u r 2 b somewhere else. (Remember last year on the 1st day when Mr. Krebb forgot 2 zip up his fly nd we LOL every time he stood up?) Dustin sits in front of me in French nd my major crush from last year is in my math class! Mile-Hi Di is now the tallest person in class. Wish u were here so I could tell u more. cya! *Posted 9/7 at 4:30 PM by ems89*

u go grl! Maybe a romance is in ur future. Sorry I can't be there for you!
Posted 9/8 at 12:16 AM by nugrl90

Wednesday, September 8

This is how the kids at my new school are different from kids at my old school:

1. A lot of them wear the color maroon. Some colors are better left in a drawer, and maroon is one of them. I guess that means they have "school spirit," but maroon socks? mmb!

2. No one has more than two piercings (that I can see), but tattoos are big—even the cheerleaders and preps have them (wonder how they got their parents to agree to that)

3. In class there are a lot more suck-ups who raise their hand whenever the teacher asks a question

4. No one seems poor

Today I talked to the cute guy who asked for help with his locker yesterday—if you can call saying "Hey" when you look at someone talking. I almost wished his lock would jam again but it didn't, so he was gone in two seconds.

Jules and I decided to grade our teachers and classes:
First Period (English)
Jules: **B–**
Ms. Gardner is pretty and young but too short to be a teacher. You can barely see or hear her from the back of the room. Plus,

she uses a lot of big words, I think to impress us.
Sadie: **C**

We all want to read *Lord of the Flies* becuz we heard there is sex in
it (and in the movie, there are hot guys), but the rest of the books
on our reading list are lame, and *Death of a Salesman* is too
depressing. WS told me all about it becuz it's a goth kind of play.
We think we should be able to pick at least one book on our own,
but Ms. Gardner says there have been *objectionable* selections
when this was an option in the past.

Second Period (Phys Ed)

Jules: **B+**

Ms. Raines seems really funny and about as good as a PE teacher
gets.

Sadie: **D**

Who wants to do anything energetic (especially field hockey) early
in the morning?

Third Period (Math)

Jules: **C**

Mr. Hammacker has distracting nose and ear hairs you can see if
you sit in the front row, and we both do. It looks like they're
exploding out of his head.

Sadie: **B**

Geometry serves no purpose in life.

Fourth Period (Lunch)
Grade deferred

We are scoping out the cafeteria to see if we want to stay at the
new table or try and fit in somewhere else. Right now it's just
me, Jules, and this other new girl, Mia, who is from Alabama and
has an accent, so sometimes I can't understand her (of course,

imagine how she feels hearing most of us speak Pennsylvaniaese—
is that a word?). No one else is real friendly, and some people even
give us the evil eye if we walk in their direction.

Today, Mia and I were waiting for Jules to get through the lunch
line, when all of a sudden Mia got kinda quiet.

"How long do you think it takes before you get used to a new
school?" she asked me in a real soft voice.

"Beats me—this is my first time," I told her, but when I tried to
get her to say more, she wouldn't, so Jules and I talked the whole
time about our favorite TV shows and music. Jules can make any
topic funny, but I felt kind of bad laughing when Mia was sitting
there so sad.

Fifth Period (History)
Jules: **A**
Hoo-rah. Mr. Lowe is gorgeous and young and smiles all the
time.
Sadie: **A**
So what if we aren't particularly interested in China?

Sixth Period (Study Period)
Grade deferred

Seventh Period (French)
Jules: **A**
Mme. Taylor would be the perfect match for Mr. Lowe—she is *très
belle*. We both want to look like her and spend a summer in
France, like she did.
Sadie: **A**

We get to make French food the first Friday of every month! I don't cook, but Mme. Taylor makes real crepes!

DAD called tonight and no one but me would talk to him. I feel like an interpreter because as soon as I get off the phone, MOM and WS ask, "What'd he say? Did he talk about his girlfriend? How did he sound?" Of course, half my conversation with DAD goes the same way. "How's your MOM? Is her new job okay?" and "How's your sister? Does she like school?"

This time, his voice sounded like it does when he has a cold and is all stuffed up, but he said it was just a bad cell-phone connection. I asked if he had gone to the West Nile Virus Information Center yet—he has not. It was a lame conversation because I mostly went o&o about nothing and he just made fatherly sounds every now and then. He told me to make sure I eat breakfast and said he wants me to come out and visit him the first chance I get. He said he has a new friend I'll really like—guess who that might be? If he is living with his *new friend* I will not even get on the plane—but I didn't tell him that.

W3TP: Students don't ever get to give teachers grades, even though we know best how good they are (or aren't).
Posted 9/8 at 5 PM

6 URock 5 ITalk

Ur site is uber-cool! I can't believe all the nice stuff you wrote about me! itz not so bad 2 eat with just u nd me nd Mia rite now! we'll have to find out who that guy is tomorrow nd make sumthin happen between the 2 of u! cya l8r
Posted 9/8 at 9 PM by nujules4u

Letz get 2gether this weekend, okay? I miss u like craze every day! My superchick sidekick is 2 far away.
Posted 9/8 at 10 PM by ems89

Hey sweetz, u r doin good! I told u 2 look on the brite side nd u did! i agree—u need 2 visit ur old friendz—urs truly included.
Posted 9/9 at 12 AM by sk8r4life

Thanks for eating with me, guys! I don't mind either if it keeps on being just the three of us—we can all be BFs and have a great year. And I agree, we should give our teachers report cards just like they do to us. Can you imagine the comments we could make: "Doesn't share belongings," "Interacts poorly with peers," "Bad attitude." As if anyone cares. In my old school we had a teacher so bad he would fall asleep reading his notes to us, and they still rehired him for the next year, even though my parents (and everyone else's) complained like crazy. My dad says educational standards in this country have reached an all-time low.

P.S. I am <u>not</u> depressed, Sadie. I just don't like it when you guys laugh at the way I talk. You may not realize it, but accents are beyond our control—I grew up in Texas (<u>not</u> Alabama), and that's the way everyone sounds there.
Posted 9/9 at 12:30 AM by kool2Bmia

Mia, I'm so sorry! I didn't mean what I wrote in a bad way, nd I like your accent—especially when you say y'all.
Posted 9/9 at 12:35 AM by nugrl90

Chapter Four

Friday, September 10

How fast you can go from hanging out at the swimming pool to a mountain of homework—on a weekend, no less. Meanwhile, WS, who is a senior and should be developing college habits, doesn't even bother bringing her books home—plus, she's been sitting out in the car and smoking (dope?) with Slap almost every afternoon before MOM gets home from work. Just because she's the oldest and the smartest and can't be bothered with the computer other than for schoolwork, she gets away with everything. Of course, MOM is in such a state these days that she sometimes goes out of the house with a curler still in her hair or with two different shoes on, so it's no wonder she's clueless about WS.

At least Aunt Sara took me to the movies for some time out after school today and <u>pretended</u> to understand how much my life sucks and how boring school is. She's a lot younger than MOM but about as different from her as me and WS.

Compare:

MOM	**Aunt Sara**
Separated from her high school sweetheart—the only BBF she ever had	Divorced three times, no kids, says she's swearing off men
Boring job (social worker at the local hospital who has to work late and do lots of meaningless paperwork)	Exciting job (freelance photo journalist who travels all around the world)
Barely making enough money to get by	Incredibly rich from her job and husband #2
Short and a little pudgy	Tall and elegantly slender
Frizzy black hair with gray streaks	Long red hair with highlights (although I don't think they're natural)

You get the picture.

W3TP: A 38-year-old woman with a job to die for, incredible looks, a red Porsche, but three divorces under her belt.
Posted 9/10 at 10:56 PM

4 URock 4 ITalk

Altho blogs are a great technologic tool to advance communication, one should not slam one's sister online, especially when she's not as bad as you make her out to be. (We don't smoke dope,

fyi. We are both opposed to drugs, except for cigs, obviously.)
Also, if your aunt hasn't been so successful at marriage, there's
nothing wrong with that, just as there is nothing wrong with
being goth.
Posted 9/10 at 11:38 PM by gr82begoth

OMG, Slap, u r 2 scary nd weird beyond belief. Sadie, he got
kicked out of school 2day 4 throwing an eraser at Mr. Krakoff's
head. He belongs with ur sister, that's 4 sure.
Posted 9/10 at 11:42 PM by ems89

Hey, I volunteered to clean up the room. Can I help it if Mr.
Wackoff falsely accused me of threatening him with an eraser? In
reality, I threw said object at the chalkboard after being bugged
about my appearance. He just happened to be standing nearby.
Posted 9/10 at 11:55 PM by gr82begoth

Let us all remember the innocent men and women who died on
this day. To see an awesome tribute go to
http://www.link4u.com/weareone.htm, which I helped create.
Pass this post on to everyone you know.
Posted 9/11 at 2 PM by 4the1swhodied

Sunday, September 12

It was really depressing in church today because of the anniversary
of 9/11. Jules says her cousin was a firefighter who was killed in
the WTC, so she came to church with me in memory of him.

Later, when I was IMing her and Mia, Jules said she was lucky to
be at her private elementary school in upper Manhattan when the
planes crashed, so she didn't see anything. Mia got all over her

case and wanted to know the name of her school and where exactly it was located. wuwt?

Even Slap and WS came to mass, and they were really serious the whole time. Afterward Slap read us a poem he wrote about bravery during times of great danger, and it was pretty good. Then MOM made the mistake of taking us out to lunch, and WS kept talking about the future of the country and blah, blah, blah. If she's so concerned, why doesn't she take off the black and blend in with the *normals* (her word)?

W3TP: WS and Slap, both in white makeup and black fishnets, sitting next to me in church.
Posted 9/12 at 3:15 PM

15 URock o ITalk

Monday, September 13

Aunt Sara came over after school because she wants to spend time with us before she goes away *on assignment* again—glamorous, huh? She is my ABSOLUTE favorite relative, forget that I don't have that many now. (Will DAD's family divorce us too?) Nana and Pap haven't even called since he moved away, but MOM says, "Give it time." Why should I? It's not like I have a lot of other relatives lined up to take their place. And I'm not the one who decided to get divorced!

Anyway, Aunt Sara took me to get my hair trimmed and then we went for ice cream and walked around the mall and discussed life. I asked her if she thought maybe I had done something to upset MOM or DAD and make them have so many problems. I know sometimes WS's goth thing and my *sensitivity* (their word) created tension, and maybe that's one of the reasons they got divorced.

Aunt Sara said, "Actually, Sadie, I consider myself a bit of an expert in this area, and sometimes people just aren't right for each other, like your MOM and DAD."

I'm not so sure she's right, though—MOM did say once that being called in to talk to the school nurse so many times really stressed her out, and even DAD hinted that my headaches were starting to give him a headache.

On the subject of MOM: these days when she gets home from working at the hospital, she's like the movie zombies that stand and stare and shift back and forth, trying to figure out what to do. She calls Aunt Sara a lot, and when they get together, they go out on the porch with a bottle of wine and two glasses—a sign they are going to be having a serious conversation about you know who. Since I felt like I was getting a headache, I went to bed instead of trying to eavesdrop.

W3TP: Two parents who get along just fine until one daughter decides to become goth and the other daughter spends half the school year in the nurse's office. I don't believe Aunt Sara.
Posted 9/13 at 9 PM

2 URock 0 ITalk

Wednesday, September 15
I am so, so, so, so, so happy!!!!

Tonight after work, MOM made me come out on the front porch with my eyes closed. Suddenly I felt this wriggly, furry body in my arms and a dry tongue started licking leftover potato-chip crumbs off my face. When I opened my eyes, I saw the most adorable dog possible—cuter than any dog I've ever seen.

"This is Homer," MOM told me. "One of the women I work with had to find a new home for him because it turned out her daughter is allergic. I know you've always wanted a dog, so . . ."

Then I was hugging her and Homer together, and he jumped free and got really excited and started barking and spinning in circles.

"Welcome to my life, Homer," I told him.

W3TP: Dogs are always happy. They never get divorced or upset, but we think they're dumber than people.
Posted 9/15 at 8:04 PM

2 URock o ITalk

Thursday, September 16

Homer is not quite the prize I first believed he would be, and maybe not be so cute either, especially at 1 AM when he was doing this jump-on-the-bed, jump-off-the-bed thing. WS threw her pillow at me and told me to take him the f*** outside because he probably had to go to the bathroom. She also said that if this was his natural personality, she was going to make sure he died a slow and painful death in the next week.

I took him outside, and he did pee, but then he just sat there on the sidewalk and stared at me with his tail wagging up and down.

"You're a bad dog," I told him in the same voice I used with the twins the time they locked me out of the house last summer. Homer didn't care. He shoved his head between my legs, not in a gross way, but in a I-want-to-be-petted way. It was too adorable.

So Homer got petted, and I got no sleep, which meant I was totally exhausted in the morning and could hardly crawl out of bed, even when MOM and WS both yelled at me.

But there are some good things about no sleep, namely:

1. Nothing bothers you the next day because you are too tired to get worked up and spend the energy being upset.

2. You know that you will fall instantly into a deep sleep as soon as you go home and your head hits the pillow.

3. You can actually fall asleep at your desk—normally impossible for me, but my head hurt so bad during 3rd period I had to try. That got me sent to the nurse's office. Unfortunately, the nurse at my new school, Ms. Penders, is not nice like Ms. Armstrong, but short and scrawny and a little mean. "Why don't your parents get you in bed at a decent hour?" she asked me. But I did get to lie down in her little private room, which is very nice, and after awhile my headache went away even though I was still really tired.

4. If you have a dog like Homer, when you come home from school and drop your backpack on the floor and crawl up to your bedroom, he follows you, and this time he stays on the bed and you both sleep.

W3TP: Sleeping like a big boat going through the world of dreams in the almost-middle of the day. Your older sister might be having sex with her BBF in the living room right below you, but you don't hear a thing.
Posted 9/16 at 10:20 PM

o URock o ITalk

Friday, September 17

I am starting to fit into my new life—I'm used to DAD not being here, and when I wake up and see WS in the bed across from me, although it's a scary sight at first, I'm not so upset by it. My school is boring and not the best, but not the worst either.

Jules and I are getting closer every day, and Mia is talking a little more, but sometimes the two of them get in these little fights about stupid things, like today when Mia asked where exactly Jules lived in NYC:

"Why do you care?" Jules asked.

"One of my cousins lives in Manhattan, and she never heard of the school you supposedly went to," Mia said.

"That's because it closed last year," Jules answered.

"And how come when I tried to find a picture of your *famous* dad, I couldn't?" Mia asked next.

"Because he happens to have a stage name for privacy," Jules said back, sort of snotty. Luckily, it was time to go to class and that ended things for today, but I wish they'd get along better.

Locker Guy has not spoken to me again, even though I try to take my books out real slow in case he shows up. Yesterday I saw him talking to a girl who was following him around like Homer does to me. I managed to take a real long drink at the fountain while observing him—try it some time, it's an excellent way to spy on someone, especially if you have longer hair and can hold it back or let it fall over your face as needed. They seemed like a lot more than friends. Sigh.

W3TP: Life without your DAD seeming normal or at least okay. Does that mean you're shallow?
Posted 9/17 at 9:06 PM

2 URock 2 ITalk

Superchick, u must b sic! wut u doin hangin out at home on a Fri nite? Come party with us, kool 1! Remember the party we had last September to decide what we wud do 4 homecoming? It totally rocked!
Posted 9/17 at 9:15 PM by ems89

You are not shallow, nor are you recovered from your father's departure, imho. Adjustment to a life crisis is like a thunderstorm—even after the rain ends, there is still water everywhere, nd sometimes broken trees. It takes time for things to grow back, nd even then, they are never the same.
Posted 9/17 at 11:03 PM by gr82bgoth

Monday, September 20

Today Jules came home with me after school and met Homer. Mia is allergic, or she would have come too, but I was sort of relieved when she couldn't because her parents are rich and live in a mansion, while I live in a falling-apart half of somebody else's house.

Unfortunately, WS was there without Slap, which meant she could focus all her energy on tormenting us, mmb. Five mean things she did:

1. Ate all the chocolate-chip cookies I made last night specifically for Jules and me

2. Put MTV on, which Jules hates, and then sat on the remote so we couldn't switch it

3. Called me *little bunnykins*

4. After she finished watching MTV, she locked herself in our bedroom so we couldn't get in to look at my pics of Emma or go online

5. Followed us out on the porch and blew cigarette smoke at us

I wish she'd go live in St. Louis with DAD. Jules was so understanding, though. She drew this hilarious picture of WS.

At least we got to take Homer on a walk by ourselves because WS doesn't want any excess exposure to sunlight. That gave us time to make plans for this weekend, when I'm going to sleep over at Jules's. I can't wait! If only Emma could come over too; it would be perfect. I know they'll like each other because we've already IMed a lot and they both like the same things: New York City, pistachio ice cream, and horror movies.

W3TP: WS. A sister is supposed to take care of you and be nice to you, like Aunt Sara and MOM or Jules and her sister.
Posted 9/20 at 11:34 PM

1 URock o ITalk

Friday, September 24
I have a horrible homework headache.

So far I am passing everything, but barely. This school is way harder than my old one, which makes me want to turn the alarm off and stay in bed in the morning. Then I realize sooner or later I have to *suck it up,* as Emma says.

Some good news, though: Locker Guy definitely looked at me this morning, and for one second I thought he was going to say something, but then his friend came over and distracted him. I tried to see his name on something—anything—but couldn't. Must discover his screen name ASAP!

Thank Someone it's Friday, and tomorrow Jules and I are going to the mall, then to a movie, and then to her house. MOM offered to finance the movie AND—don't fall over—WS is going to drive us. As bad as she is, she's still better than a parent driving you places. Sometimes she even lets me pick the radio station, but only sometimes, and usually I have to sit in the backseat. Lest you think she is a decent person, she is only allowed to borrow DAD's car as long as she helps MOM with driving, so her motivation is suspect.

W3TP: Hours of homework every night. It doesn't make you smarter; it causes brain overload.
Posted 9/24 at 7:16 PM

2 URock 1 ITalk

Hey superslick superchick—when teachers load up the books, give 'em nasty looks. Remember how we used 2 do that last year nd eventually they got the message!

Glad 2 hear u r moving on with ur life nd making new friends, altho we will be VVBFs 4 ever. u'll never guess who invited me over 4 the weekend—Mile-Hi Di. She plays field hockey too, so we have been hanging out some. Since u left, I have zero friends! (sound of ♥ breaking.) Speaking of field hockey, we have a big game 2morrow, so I'm off 2 bed. Think of me!
Posted 9/24 at 10 PM by ems89

Sunday, September 26

Last night, Jules and I stayed up until 3 in the morning, and she told me her entire life story, which is way more interesting than mine. To begin with, her dad is such a famous opera singer, he travels all around the world for shows and is making a CD. Jules has a picture of him—from the newspaper, no less! He's so handsome, much more than my DAD, but a little beefy, which I guess is the way opera stars are.

Her mom is an ex-model who is writing a book about being the daughter of a millionaire and wife of a world-famous singer! Actually, she is a hand model, so if you see a picture of a pretty hand wearing a watch or bracelet or ring in a magazine, it could be her mom's. Jules says her mom used to always wear gloves and wouldn't do anything that would risk hurting her hands, like push Jules on the swings in the park or go swimming. She also says her mom isn't really that smart, so it takes all of her effort for her to concentrate on writing the book. That's another reason why Jules lives with her sister, Mona, who has a 3-year-old daughter, Abby.

Abby is too cute! Her dad doesn't live around here, so the three of them are kind of on their own. But Jules is so lucky to have an awesome older sister and a cute little niece.

When I went to New York City with the French Club last year to see *Les Mis*, I thought I would never in a million years be able to live someplace so crowded and dirty, but Jules says there are other parts of the city that are really nice: the penthouse where her parents live, for example. She promised I could come along when she goes home for a visit sometime, and since Emma adores NYC, she could come too.

Unlike me, Jules had so many boyfriends at her old school that all the girls were jealous and made problems for her constantly. She says in New York it doesn't matter if you're beautiful or not; there are other reasons that boys like you, like for having a killer sense of fashion or being a good poet or really smart.

Jules has what my DAD calls *interesting* looks, which are the kind that stick in your mind for a long time after you see them. Here's a self-portrait of her playing her BBF's guitar.

I'm not even lucky enough to look interesting, but DAD used to tell me that "Many a Plain Jane grew into a Stunning Sue." He's corny like that and you can see how it affected WS—she became a goth just to prove him wrong.

Jules might actually have it a little worse than me because she isn't living with either of her parents, and she and Mona and Abby are temporarily squashed together in this apartment with one bedroom. (We slept in the living room on the floor.)

I wish I had a niece, although if I ever get one, she'll probably be dressed completely in black. Abby loves to give hugs, and if you think of everything cute a little girl could be, she is it. We didn't even mind when she brought her blanket and pillow out to sleep with us.

We stayed up so late, I came home and crashed immediately. Of course, MOM woke me up and sent me off to evening mass with WS. What a big joke.

W3TP: A friend with a way famous family in a nowhere town

like this.
Posted 9/26 at 8:19 PM

---

1 URock 6 ITalk

i had fun too. u r so different from kids in NYC, but u r still cool, nd I can't wait to meet Emma. i kno she will still be ur VBF, even tho u moved away. Emma, Sades misses u so much!
Posted 9/26 at 11:30 PM by nujules4u

I thought you guys told me you were too busy to do anything this weekend! If there's one thing I can't stand, it's liars, especially when they're dumb enough to get caught. Don't you know I read your blog too, Sadie? It so happens my parents just got me my own laptop so I can go online anywhere now.
Posted 9/26 at 11:45 PM by kool2Bmia

xcuse me if I happen to live in a small apartment nd can only have 1 person sleep over at a time nd don't live in a big mansion lik u!
Posted 9/26 at 11:50 PM by nujules4u

Mia, she's just kidding and I'm so sorry—we didn't want to hurt your feelings. It really is true that for right now Jules has to live in a place that is only big enough for one person to stay over.
Posted 9/26 at 11:55 PM by nugrl90

You two deserve each other—I've had enough of trying to be friends with losers who can't even afford to live in a real house with a normal family.
Posted 9/26 at 11:56 PM by kool2Bmia

u suck big time, Mia! u r the 1 who needs 2 get a life nd stop sticking ur big nose in2 mine. my sister told me about the time u called nd pretended u wanted 2 talk 2 me, but rilly just wanted to try nd find out stuff about our family.

Posted 9/26 at 11:59 PM by nujules4u

Chapter Five

Monday, September 27

News flash: our so-called friendship with Mia is over. Me and Jules and her IMed back and forth like crazy after those last posts. Then this morning at school the two of them got in a big word war, and Mia threatened to show a printout of the whole conversation to our principal.

Worst of all, Locker Guy was there when it happened. I didn't even notice him until he kind of nudged me and asked if I knew what was going on. After I told him a little bit about the *unfortunate event* he shook his head and said, "People think guys are intense because we get in so many fights, but girls are the ones who just can't let go."

I have to admit he's right, even though he left before I could say anything else. Things did get a little extreme between Mia and Jules— I've had a major headache ever since this started (though I'm still avoiding the nurse). Mia, since I know you'll read this: I really did like you, but your comment about my family wasn't very nice.

Speaking of whom . . . tonight DAD and MOM went o&o over the phone about T-Day (Thanksgiving). WS had to turn her music up extra loud to drown out MOM's yelling. Then she opened the bedroom window and smoked a cigarette, right there! When I coughed *politely* to let her know how obnoxious it was, she just lit another. And she has two hickeys on her neck—tgfw.

After the phone call was over, MOM came up and sat on my bed, weeping. I felt so sorry for her. Apparently DAD wants both me and WS to go out to St. Louis for Thanksgiving and spend our entire vacation there. He also wants to have us there for half of Xmas. WS just said w/e and shrugged her shoulders, but I could see her face turning red like it does when we get in a really big fight.

The more MOM talked, the more upset she got. DAD also wants her to pay for half of our plane tickets. We barely have enough money as it is, even though DAD tells me he sends more child support and alimony than he has to. Maybe he forgets how expensive it is for two teenaged girls to live these days, especially when their MOM has a *noble but low-paying job* (Aunt Sara's description). I know I will be wearing my winter coat from last year again, even if the zipper is broken.

Tomorrow I'm going to look for a job so I can help out, but if I have to go to St. Louis for Thanksgiving vacation, who will hire me? I offered to give MOM the $47 I had left from babysitting last summer, but that just made her snot cry.

W3TP: A MOM who is so sad she doesn't even notice her daughter's hickey.
Posted 9/27 at 11:02 PM

0 URock, 1 ITalk

Hey, cheer up girl! U rilly shud come to my church with me. It rockz!
Posted 9/27 at 11:30 PM by sk8r4life

Wednesday, September 29

The only way I will EVER be in church with Dustin (whose initials are DUB—one letter short of DUMB) is if our funerals are at the same time. I wish he'd take a hint! As they say on one of my DAD's stupid old records: "Hey, hey, you, you, get off of my cloud!" Isn't it enough that he gets to hang out with my old friends while I'm stuck here in a new school?

Three Reasons Not to Like Dustin:
1. His main interest in life is skateboarding, so any girl dating him will always end up sitting and watching and watching and watching unless she is convinced to skateboard too—in which case she'll break her arm, and he'll break up with her.

2. When you break up (even if he dumped you), he will stalk you online. And don't bother blocking him from your buddy list, becuz he will only change his screen name again and again.

3. His screen names are so lame: ibesk8tin, u4me990, JCNME04, LUVTHLRD04.

W3TP: "Christians" who post stalker ITalks on their x-girlfriend's blog.
Posted 9/29 at 3:23 PM

1 URock 6 ITalk

u r in the kno, add that he wears ugly clothes. 2day at lunch he spilled ketchup on his shirt nd when everyone laughed at him, he left our table to go sit with Di.
Posted 9/29 at 4:15 PM by ems89

Reasons why a girl (like me) thinks Dustin is awesome:
He is incredibly buff
He takes you on real dates, not just meet-me-there or crowd dates
He never gets angry or upset
He is a God-fearing young man
Posted 9/29 at 5:30 PM by milhidi

Di, u have ur head in the sky. we can't be friends if u date Sadie's x-guy. (plus u r like 2 feet taller than him.)
Posted 9/29 at 5:35 PM by ems89

Emma, wutz up with the rhyming? nd y do u care so much that I like Dustin?
Posted 9/29 at 5:40 PM by milhidi

WHATEVER!
Posted 9/29 at 5:43 PM by ems89

As an fyi: ur dad hung up on me every time I called after u broke ur arm.
Posted 9/29 at 6 PM by sk8r4life

Thursday, September 30

Di, you are in for a surprise. I used to think he was wonderful but believe me he's not. Read my blog! But I am so over him, I don't care at all if you want to go out with him. Warning—don't get on his skateboard!

But enough about Dustin, more about Locker Guy or my very own Buff Boy (BB). (Jules and I decided this is a far better name and it happens to be true.) (It also happens that his real name is Brian B: majorly significant.)

Jules is too much—today she actually came up to me at my locker and kind of pushed me into him. At first he looked mad, but then he saw how embarrassed I was, so he said he was sorry, and I said I was sorry, and we just started talking until the bell rang.

THEN, I was walking out of school at the end of the day and OMG—there he was! He saw me and waited to walk out with me—thankfully I had on my best jeans (the ones Emma helped me pick out because they are tight in all the right places—her words).

We were almost to the lobby when, horror of horrors, WS started coming toward me because we ride home together every day, and I knew my relationship with BB could be over before it even got started. She looked so totally weird. She had on elbow-high black gloves, a knee-length black petal skirt, combat boots, fishnets, and a "Take a Stab at Me" T-shirt. (Sad to say, this is one of her conservative outfits.) Kids at our new school are really picky about appearances, but even at our old school I sometimes got grief because of the way WS looked.

Anyway, I guess she saw my eyes squint like they do when I am especially upset with her, so she sort of swerved off to the side and mouthed something about waiting in the car. I'm sure she was thrilled for the opportunity to smoke a cigarette before we drove home.

AMAZINGLY, <u>BB asked for my phone number</u> and said he thought we should get together sometime! I really ntk if he is serious about that other girl I saw him with, because one thing I will not do is date someone who is with someone else. How to find out though? He doesn't seem like the kind of person to be dishonest. He's too sweet and sensitive, I can tell already. (Don't ask me how.)

And when will he call? When is <u>sometime</u>?

When I told Jules that I wished I had a picture of him, she drew this.

Now, before I go to sleep, I look at it and hope I will dream about my to-die-for, handsome BB all night.

<u>W3TP: Tension-excitement-attraction-fear-happiness—how can one person cause so many different feelings in another person?</u>
Posted 9/30 at 8:02 PM

---

o URock 2 ITalk

i remember when u felt that way about me. im sorry u r finding sumone else. i guess i will move on 2, but u r my 1st

luv, nd 4 the record, Di nd me are just friends.
Posted 9/30 at 5 PM by sk8r4life

OMG, i feel lik a matchmaker! u 2 will be so cute 2gether. my
BBF from NYC called tonite and he is so missing me. Not sure if
i told u about him, he has a band called Way 2 Cool and a big
record-label person wants to hear them play. Wudn't that be 2
Cool? (hee hee)?
Posted 9/30 at 10:03 PM by nujules4u

Monday, October 4

I have been sick with the flu since Friday, when I stayed home
from school. You don't want to know the details. It's probably a
good thing that BB hasn't called me. Tomorrow I will go back to
school, but in the meantime, Jules got all my work and gave it to
WS. If you ever think about staying home from school because
you aren't feeling that hot, don't do it. I can't even figure out
most of my homework, so I will probably have to stay after today,
which will *infuriate* WS because she has to wait around for me.

Infuriate: to enrage or incite, a.k.a. the story of my life with WS. It
isn't enough that she's smarter and prettier than me. Our baby
pictures will show this is true, and even now if you scraped off
her makeup and put her in normal clothes and took the purple
dye out of her hair, she would still look way better than me. But
I am the youngest, so I got more attention and that is what
probably started the whole infuriation thing.

WS became a goth at my age when her VBF decided to try it.
(Thank you, Emma, for sparing me such a fate!) Here I am two
years later with a sister whose wardrobe is 90 percent black, and

who even went to prom in a black dress with a lot of metal on it. Sometimes MOM tells her it is depressing to see her always in black, and once Dad said he would give her $10 to wear pink for a day. (She wouldn't do it.)

But last year, in one of their rare shows of unity, MOM and DAD said if the worst thing she did was wear black, they wouldn't complain. Now, I bet they wouldn't care if WS dyed her skin purple—all they do is fight with each other. (Isn't that why they split up?) DAD doesn't even talk to me that much when he calls because he wants to get right to the big argument with MOM about Thanksgiving. His occasional emails are all about how terrible it must be for us living with someone like her. Gee thanks, Dad.

I told WS neither of them really care where we spend Thanksgiving as long as they have something they can scream at each other about. She just blew cigarette smoke at me and said I need to get over it. a/i she is.

But maybe if they really do get divorced it will do some good for WS; she actually made me chicken soup yesterday and brought it upstairs on a box lid because she couldn't find a tray. A rare event—WS being nice.

I can only remember three other times:
1. In second grade I fell on the sidewalk on the way to school, and she used her white(!) skirt to wipe the blood off my knees.

2. In fifth grade when I didn't get a harmonica for Xmas like I asked, she bought me one with her allowance money.

3. Last year she tried to fix me up with Slap's brother who is my age (a world-class nerd, but I was upset about Dustin and she was trying to help).

So, including the soup, that's four nice things in fifteen years. Emma and Jules have older sisters who are nice all the time—what did I do to get WS?

W3TP: Homer has slept right in my face all week and he is healthy as ever, while MOM told Aunt Sara that I was *as sick as a dog.*
Posted 10/4 at 11:30 PM

8 URock 4 ITalk

u r so rite about sisters, they can be cool and then cruel—don't be fooled. 1 time my sister cornrowed my hair, which took 3 hours, nd it looked so good nd i was so happy, until i found out she got orange nail polish on my fav shirt nd was just trying to distract me.
Posted 10/4 at 11:34 PM by ems89

i'm so glad u will be in school 2morrow, im tired of eating lunch without u! 2day I had 2 sit dangerously close to Mia's *new* table. All she does is brag about how rich her dad is. Someone shud tell him 2 buy her btr clothes. . . .
Posted 10/4 at 11:45 PM by nujules4u

You don't have any room to criticize me when you wear things that look like you fished them OUT OF THE TRASH. Why don't you buy some nice clothes since your parents are supposedly so rich? Every time I see you, all I can think is: BARGAIN BASEMENT REJECTS!
Posted 10/4 at 11:55 PM by kool2Bmia

w/e. if u tried u could have a whole nu look that doesn't scream out "i'm a wannabe prep." Sades, plz come to school 2day!
Posted 10/5 at 6:55 AM by nujules4u

Tuesday, October 5

You can tell I am the kind of person who hates fighting. When Emma and I were little, if we got in an argument I would get such a terrible headache I couldn't get out of bed.

The Mia saga continues. She and Jules are still in this major cyberslam and it's driving me crazy. If you're reading this, Mia, Jules didn't really mean it when she IMed that you're fat and have a bad complexion—she gets in bad moods sometimes. Like this morning, for example, when she told me my shirt was lame and pointed out the big flaw I hadn't noticed when I bought it at the outlet. Someday she will design clothes because she is really picky about stuff like that. Anyway, everyone has their own sense of style. I have been called *retro jock.* Who knows what that means?

W3TP: When two girls who used to be friends use all their energy to become worst enemies.
Posted 10/5 at 4 PM

o URock 3 ITalk

f*** you, Sadie, and Jules too. You both have major attitude. I have lots of other friends, as you can see now that I stopped eating at the loser table with you. Girls who don't appreciate what another girl has to offer are lacking in self-esteem, according to my mom, who works in pediatrics.
Posted 10/5 at 4:10 PM by kool2Bmia

i don't care wut Sadie says, i'm glad u don't eat with us nemore. i only pre1oed to be ur friend because of her.
Posted 10/5 at 4:15 PM by nujules4u

Ladies, ladies—MEOW! Why must you fight so? Appearance is only a whisper of the person inside.
Posted 10/5 at 5:30 PM by gr82bgoth

Wednesday, October 6

Well, as you can see, my friendships are a little complicated right now, but to be honest, I don't care because . . . TODAY, BB gave me a note when we passed in the hallway. It said:

New Girl:
Although others may call me tough
Since you arrived I stopped being rough
You have eyes like copper pennies
The things I like about you are many
Why don't you just give me a chance
And go with me Friday to the dance?

OMG. I couldn't believe it when I read it. Jules and I were both screaming in the bathroom, but then Mme. Taylor came in and said, "Ladies, *n'est pas l'heure diner?*" or something like that, so I shoved the note in my pocket and went to lunch.

He called me as soon as I got home from school and we talked for like an hour! He told me the girl I saw him with is his BF Ronzo's cousin—can you believe it? Now the poem is under my pillow, and I can't stop thinking about what to wear to the dance.

W3TP: A boy who's called a tough guy writing me a poem?
Posted 10/6 at 5 PM

10 URock 4 ITalk

Brian Boynes's "poetry" sucks! And that boy is trouble—just looking at him should give you a clue. How many tattoos does he have? My friends all tell me he is BAD NEWS. Even though you ditched me I feel sorry for you because you are so clueless, which is why I'm even bothering to write. P.S. Your "friends" (one in particular) are world-class jerks.
Posted on 10/6 at 5:10 PM by kool2Bmia

Jealous: to be envious of and covet. Does the shoe fit, Mia?
Posted 10/6 at 5:15 PM by nujules4u

Poetry is the window to the soul. It matters not how well written—'tis the thought behind the words.
Posted 10/6 at 5:30 PM by gr82bgoth

Superchick, I luv his note—it's the sweetest thing a guy ever wrote. I wish I was u, I prolly wouldn't be blue. Di nd Dustin r definitely together now. And no one has time 4 me. Thankfully, our field hockey team is in first place nd I haven't missed a shot yet! I'll call u after practice. Miss u!
Posted 10/6 at 6 PM by ems89

Thursday, October 7
Why is it that when you really need something incredible to wear, you can't find it? I tried on every outfit in my closet for the dance tomorrow night and nothing looks right. Do I want the clean,

all-American-girl look, or the sweet, semi-slut look? Jock is definitely out. One look I know I don't want is goth, and that rules out just about everything WS owns, except one really hot red shirt that I so covet. But she keeps it locked in the car trunk because she knows I like it.

Homer is oblivious, just lying across my feet and not caring that every article of clothing I own is thrown around the room. When WS came in, she took one look and then left in a snit, slamming the door as hard as she could so I would know she was pissed. a/i! She <u>always</u> uses my bed as her personal trash can.

brb, Aunt Sara is here.

Later: Aunt Sara said MOM was working late and she was there to take me and WS out to eat. Lucky for me, WS had already driven off with her beloved Slap, so I asked if we could go to the mall instead.

DAD sent me $50 last week, probably because he feels guilty, and after going through my nonexistent wardrobe, I had no doubt what that money was meant to be spent on: a special BB knock-your-socks-off outfit. So, Aunt Sara and me ate stuffed pizza until we were stuffed, then we shopped a little, but not at the stores where the *popular* girls go. Aunt Sara took me to these cute little places with unusual names like "Your Auntie's Bottom Drawer" and "Lost and Found." It took about an hour but I found IT, the perfect outfit. Even Aunt Sara agreed.

- Top: cream-colored satin with just the right amount of lace to accent the cleavage I don't have (must sneak MOM's most padded bra)

- Bottom: Faded blue jeans with satin ribbons woven through the hem

- Accessories: Aunt Sara offered to lend me her special pearl choker and crystal drop earrings

- Shoes: MOM has a pair of mini boots she never wears that I already know fit me

Now it's midnight and I am so excited I can't sleep, just thinking about BB, every curve of his face and the way his eyes get even darker and bluer when he smiles and they crinkle up. He has a nice straight nose and a jaw that is a little square, but not too much.

What will I say when I see him on Friday, less than 24 hours away? OMG, OMG. tefw! I called DAD to tell him all about it, but I got his answering machine like a million times, and MOM is working late—again.

Forget WS. My happiness would only incite her (as explained previously).

I am so totally freaked! I need mindless distraction—thank you, Emma, for forwarding this. (Remember the first dance last year, when we wore our hair in mega ponytails?)

GO ALONG OR STAY HOME?
School: Stay home
Church: Depends
Friend's house: Go, go, go—anytime, anyplace, anywhere
Topless beach: Stay home! (Are you kidding?)

Foreign country: Go, but not alone

Trick-or-treating: Regretfully, stay home

MOST _____ I'VE DONE

Stupid thing: Fell off a skateboard when it wasn't moving

Daring thing: Snuck out of my room one night to see my ex-BBF

Secret thing: I'd rather put it in a newspaper headline (a/i!)

Happy thing: Hanging out with Emma and eating ice cream

Funny thing: Trying to put cool blue streaks in my hair but ending up with solid blue smurf hair (oh wait, that wasn't me, that was WS)

Romantic thing: Sitting through six hours of a skateboard competition wearing a T-shirt that says "Dustin will bust 'em."

<u>**W3TP: Boys can wear jeans and a T-shirt and look just fine, but girls have to go for the whole deal: earrings, shirt, pants or skirt, shoes, etc., not to mention hairstyle.**</u>

Posted 10/7 at 11:58 PM

2 URock 1 ITalk

i wish i could b there 4 u, superchick—I'd make u look great real quick. Yes, i remember the ponytails! nd do u remember how we did each other's hair 4 homecoming last year? U looked 2 beautiful!

Posted 10/7 at 11:59 PM by ems89

Chapter Six

Saturday, October 9

Yesterday I felt like I was going to hurl. I couldn't eat lunch, which is rare—usually I'm ravenous and even scarf Jules's leftovers. All I could talk about was the dance and what I should say when I meet up with BB. BB, of course, is still in the brand-new stage and can't compare to Jules's BBF and his band and the CD they just cut, which she promised to burn for me so we can both memorize every song. Jules was so sweet and said when she is nervous she tells herself something her mother wrote for her book: "Believe in yourself and so will everyone else."

But I still got butterflies when I passed BB in the hallway and he winked at me and said, "See you later, Sadie."

If I was at my old school with my old life all this would be easier, imho. With Dustin and me, we hung out together because a lot of our friends knew each other. Now I only have one real friend at my new school, and BB is so gorgeous it scares me. . . . I wouldn't be surprised to turn on the TV someday in the future and see him starring in some famous show, probably an action movie, because he has so many muscles and likes to fool around and air box with his friends.

So anyway, this is what happened at the dance: when Jules and I got there, BB was waiting for me right inside the door with a smile all sweet and funny. He looked so cute in his dark blue T-shirt, which matched his eyes perfectly. It felt like a magnet was pulling me closer and closer to him.

He asked me to dance, and of course he is a great dancer, especially because he was a little drunk. We danced every dance, fast and slow, and I felt so sexy, even though he is a way better dancer than me. When the DJ took a break, BB kind of folded me up inside his jacket and kissed me, and I'm sure everyone in the school wondered, what is that new girl doing with someone as gorgeous and wonderful as he is? The chaperones hustled over and scolded us—not even noticing that BB's friends were falling down drunk.

We went outside with his friends after that, and I felt like I finally had a real place at our new school. Lots of younger guys hung around BB, which would usually be a bad thing, but I can tell he's accepting like that. I didn't say much (they were talking about some computer game they all play), but with BB's arm around me, I belonged.

BB was passing around a bottle of apricot brandy he took from his mom's liquor cabinet, and pretty soon it was gone. I tried a swallow but immediately choked, which he thought was hilarious.

Then we went back in and danced, and when one of BB's friends tried to dance with me, BB shoved him so hard he fell down, right on the gym floor. The chaperone, who happened to be Mr. Hammacker, came running over, but we were all laughing and BB said it was a joke, so he left us alone.

As upset as I've been because of the move, that's how happy I feel when I'm with BB. I didn't even know where Jules was this whole time because I felt like I was in a dream, just melting against BB until there was no me or him, just us. When it was over, he walked me outside and we stood and kissed(!), and then at the last minute, I remembered MOM was going to pick me up because WS couldn't.

I almost died right there. She witnessed the whole thing, and as expected, she started the inquisition the moment I got into the car:

Did you have a good time?

Who was there?

Where's Jules?

Who was that boy?

How did you meet him?

What do his parents do?

Where does he live?

She went o&o with the personal questions about BB, but mostly I just said I don't know, because I really don't know that much about those things. I could care less what his parents do—it's the way he kisses I can't stop thinking about.

When we got home she asked why I was so grouchy; if she only listened to her own questions she would know. Inside I was so wishing she hadn't been there on time so I could have kissed BB again and again before I had to leave. MOM finally went to bed and left me alone, but I bet she gets up in a few minutes and tells me to turn off the computer and go to bed too.

Sure enough, here she comes.

W3TP: Drinking something that tastes like medicine, just becuz it's booze.
Posted 10/9 at 1:30 AM

5 URock 1 ITalk

Don't worry about me, i had a gr8 time by myself when u ditched me to go outside with those guyz. Sometimes u rilly r clueless, Sadie, and just becuz i have a BBF, he is in NYC far away nd that doesn't mean i don't get lonely too—or that it doesn't bother me to be ditched at a dance!

After u nd BB starting making out rite in front of me, i just left, and if u remember, ur mom was going 2 give me a ride home, but no matter, i walked.
Posted on 10/9 at 2 AM by nujules4u

Tuesday, October 12
Ugh, my bad. What was I thinking? Jules and me had a serious

fight about the dance, and she is right. I shouldn't have left her, because she is new too and didn't know anyone and ended up by herself. How would I feel in the same situation?

As soon as I read her post I called, even though it was early and Mona got mad at me. Jules wouldn't talk to me then, or the three other times I tried, until I apologized again and again and finally she accepted.

Yesterday, just to be extra nice, I had WS drive us to the mall after school, and we hung out all day. I think Jules finally got the message that I did a stupid thing and was genuinely sorry for it. When I told her that me and BB are officially together now, and that he's only my second real boyfriend and how much I care about him already, she said she remembered feeling the same way about her BBF.

BB called when I got home from the mall, and we talked for two hours! He told me about his life and how rotten our school is (because the teachers all suck), and I told him how my parents are in the midst of World War 3 over their divorce, which should be something they're happy about. He is such a good listener that it made me wish we could talk all night, but MOM made me hang up, courtesy of WS.

Thankfully, WS is now away with MOM looking at schools for next year. (They better make sure to find a university where the school color is black.) I told Aunt Sara about what happened with Jules when she drove me to school today, and she said maybe I just miss having a guy around—of course she means my DAD—but I don't agree, because you can't replace a parent with a boyfriend, and I could never talk on the phone with DAD for two hours.

Aunt Sara reads a lot of books about parenting, even though she doesn't have kids. When I asked her why, she said it's so she can be helpful to me and WS. Isn't that totally sweet? She talks about how common divorce is and how the main thing is to *express my feelings* about it. I told her sometimes I drink orange juice for breakfast because I can't stand to remember me and DAD with our stupid Frooty Loops, and she nodded just like MOM does in therapist mode and said that is exactly the kind of thing I need to talk about.

Big news: In two weeks BB's mom is going away for most of the weekend and Jules says I can tell MOM I'm staying with her. (It's not really sneaking because I will spend part of the time with her.) BB is going to throw a party and only invite people who are really cool, which excludes most of our school (superchick to superchick: rhyming is fun!).

Words that describe how I feel about BB:

Soap bubbles

Cotton candy

Tingles

Heart beat, beat, beat

Those puffy white clouds on top of each other in the sky

Some other things I love about him already: he reads lots of books about martial arts and space travel, and he totally understands how I feel about WS and MOM and DAD. He says I just have to find happiness elsewhere. It's been two years since his parents split, and he says now it doesn't really matter that his dad remarried someone with a bunch of little kids (stepsiblings—eeww).

W3TP: Gothic universities.
Posted 10/12 at 3:34 PM

o URock 2 ITalk

Boy, u r hooked! u kno that song my BBF wrote 4 me, maybe I didn't play it 4 u, but it's all about the way u feel on ur birthday when it's special all day nd u can do anything u want and no 1 cares? He sez that's how I make him feel every day. Hehe. u remind me of that.

i'm so glad we made up. u r the BF a grl could ever have, nd altho i miss my mom nd dad (who are in Australia rite now), i'm glad 2 have u.
Posted on 10/12 at 9:20 PM by nujules4u

Aww . . . that's just too cute, Jules. Your BBF loves you so much! I can't wait to meet him. I do wish I had a BBF who could write songs about me and send me presents all the time like yours does, but I know BB will make it big for something one day, and I will be at his side.
Posted on 10/12 at 9:36 PM by nugrl90

Wednesday, October 13
Isn't it funny how love is so different for each person? I think WS probably loves Slap in her own way, but you would never know it

watching her order him around the way she does. I guess I understand it, though, because I would do almost anything BB asked me to, just to make him happy. I can't believe how much I care about him already! Love is like that. . . .

I am so glad Jules and me made up and we're VBF again. Every girl needs at least two VBFs—I'm lucky! btw, Emma, I haven't forgotten about you! I didn't mean to blow you off on the phone last night but I really was on the other line with BB. It's our only way to communicate right now. Please answer my calls!

W3TP: Friendships are a good thing—why are they so hard?
Posted 10/13 at 4:03 PM

1 URock 4 ITalk

If sumone is ur VBF, they will stick by u until death. Just becuz BB doesn't believe in communicating online like normal ppl do shud not b a problem 2 a friendship. But w/e, u were like this with Dustin 2, nd u got over it when u discovered how he rilly was.
Posted 10/13 at 5:06 PM by ems89

Emma, 'member how Sadie left me at the dance? i wuz pissed too, but then i realized that once i did the same thing to my VBF at my old school. u hav a beautiful friendship—don't let it die!!
Posted 10/13 at 5:30 PM by nujules4u

WS tells me that girls don't make good friends becuz they will fight with you over a BBF. When she started going out with Slap, she lost a lot of her VBFs becuz they didn't appreciate her behavior. (Of course, it's amazing she even had VBFs before

Slap.) Point being—this will not happen to us. I luv the two of you like sisters and wish you were here to balance out the gothmeister.
Posted 10/13 at 5:45 PM by nugrl90

hey, wut about me? . . . psych!
Posted 10/13 at 6 PM by sk8r4life

Chapter Seven

Saturday, October 16

This morning I woke up and had a glimpse of WS dashing out of our bedroom door wearing my favorite shirt: the plain white one she calls *Catholic school girl dropout.* Aunt Sara gave it to me as a *cheer up* present when she came back from London last summer, but I've only worn it a few times because I wanted to save it for ykw.

I flew out of bed in time to tackle WS and demand that she TAKE OFF MY SHIRT RIGHT NOW (in those words, more or less), just as MOM shuffled out of her bedroom in her ratty old teddy bear pj's and told me to let it go. Something about the tone of her voice and the way WS looked (no black makeup, hair in a pony-tail, and no leather or plastic or other gruesome stuff) made me back off.

It turned out that WS was on her way to meet Slap's grandmother—can you believe it? I can just imagine a goth grandmother, with black lipstick and totally white hair—tafw.

Without WS around to torment me, it was pretty boring. MOM had a bunch of divorce papers to work on, so I left her alone because I knew she would really start crying if I bugged her. That's the way she's been lately. The upside is she's forgotten about BB for the time being and doesn't bug me with stupid questions—or notice that I'm actually happy!

I decided to make Homer my project for the day, so I dragged him into the bathroom. If you have ever wrestled a 60-pound dog into a very small bathtub, you will understand what a challenge it was. I got him all wet and soapy till he looked about 20 pounds lighter, and both of us had had a bath by the time it was done.

The most amazing thing about dogs is that they have no memory. WS and me have had some terrible fights: throwing books and pans at each other, wrestling on the floor, screaming that we hate each other so much we think we can never live in the same house again, and it takes days before we even speak to each other. Homer, on the other hand, forgot the trauma of his bath once it was done, and he wagged his tail and plopped his head down on my lap like I was his VBF ever.

After that I was bored again, so we went for a long walk, and you won't believe it, but at the 7-Eleven where I stopped for a soda, BB was there with one of his friends. Even though he never met BB before, Homer jumped up and put his paws on BB's shoulders and shoved his doggy face right into BB's. Homer's tail was wagging so hard his whole body was vibrating. Who could resist that? Not BB—he ended up leaving his friend and walking us home, which was not easy because Homer is so lacking in the obedience department you can barely control him, even with a leash.

I didn't want MOM to see BB and give me the third degree again, so I said good-bye at the corner and we kissed behind a tree for a few minutes, until Homer jerked me away. Tonight we are going to meet up at the movies if BB can get a ride. (Me and Jules and Emma already made plans for a sleepover at my house after the movie, so I can finally introduce them.)

This is what I else I have learned about BB:

- His smile is a whole-face smile.
- His dad is a cop in Philadelphia who married a doctor that makes lots of $. She expects BB's dad to take care of her four kids but refuses to let BB visit very often because his tattoos are a *bad influence.*
- BB's dad gives BB a hard time by yelling at him over the phone and trying to dictate to his mom what BB should and shouldn't do. (Maybe I should be glad my DAD is in a state of oblivion over his new girlfriend and only calls once a week.)
- Last year BB got detention six times for *bad behavior,* but only because Ms. Turner, the principal, is a dickhead (BB is not the only one to tell me this about Ms. T).
- Since sixth grade he has gotten all A's, but it's really not a big deal because our school is *boring and way too easy* (his words, obviously). Most of the time in class he thinks about the new computer game he wants to create starring a martial arts hero who goes back in time.
- His dog ran away last year, and his mom refuses to get another one because she says BB never took care of it. (I told him I hear similar complaints and he can *borrow* Homer any time he wants.)
- The only thing he does on the computer is play games because his dad works in computer crimes and has the habit of checking up on him online.

I can't wait until BB's mom goes away! Must start planning soon!

W3TP: An awesome guy who's too smart for school and gets treated so unfairly by just about everyone!
Posted 10/16 at 4:09 PM

---

10 URock 2 ITalk

Um hello, Ms. Superclueless. BB is the biggest troublemaker in school—that's all everyone at my lunch table talks about, because he went out with one of my new BF's sisters last year. She broke up with him because he was too weird. You ntk what you are getting into, even though we're not friends anymore.
Posted 10/16 at 10:10 PM by kool2Bmia

Mia, u r 2 much. U must be turning green while u rite this because u r so jealous.
Posted 10/16 at 11 PM by nujules4u

Sunday, October 17

Some girls really go out of their way to hurt other people. I can't understand why Mia resents my relationship with BB. Anyway . . . I won't tell everything that happened with BB last night at the movies, but let's just say it wasn't easy giving my MOM the details of the plot on the way home. Emma and Jules were practically splitting with laughter in the backseat when I was trying to answer her questions. It was tffw.

It ended up being an absolutely perfect evening/night. Emma and Jules really liked each other. After the movie we spent all night talking and laughing and raiding the refrigerator. (We slept in the living room to avoid WS.)

Today was a snore! After Emma and Jules left, MOM made me go
to mass with her. I slept through it when she wasn't elbowing
me. This time WS went too, and as usual, all the old ladies were
turning around to stare at her. Maybe it was her fishnet shirt, or
the silver tank top underneath? Or could it have been her black
plastic pants? I can tell it made MOM kind of embarrassed too.
Parents ntk that kids aren't going to be uber religious just cause
you drag them to church every Sunday, or every other Sunday.

After church MOM took us out for breakfast, even though she
knows I hate to appear in public with WS. (It's one thing to be new
and have to make your way in school; it's another thing completely
to be new and have the queen of goth paving the way for you.)

So there I was eating my blueberry pancakes, when MOM's agenda
became clear. She launched into this whole discussion of birth
control, acting like the touchy-feely social worker she is. Luckily, our
table was far away from everyone else's. It was so embarrassing
and way tmi, especially when she talked about how she too had a
sweetheart when she was my age.

Meanwhile, WS kept smirking at me from behind her napkin or
nodding her head and saying, "You're so right, Mo" (her nickname for MOM). Two years ago, WS was *nice* enough to
describe in detail (and I mean nothing left to the imagination)
what sex is like, so I already knew all the stuff MOM was telling
me. In addition to the sex talk, MOM added some of her favorite
questions, which she asks me just about every day and which I'm
sure are right out of her therapy books:

How does it really feel to be new, Sadie? Tell me a word that comes into your head when you think about it. My answer: Blisters. I didn't explain to her that what I meant was that going to this school has been like wearing a new pair of shoes that are a little too small: at first you might get a blister, which makes your shoes hurt you more, but eventually you get used to them, and soon they're just like your old comfy shoes—at least I'm hoping that's what happens.

What are you feeling about your father? How has his abandonment of the family affected you? My answer to this one is a complete lie, of course: "I want Daddy to be happy, but please stop buying Frooty Loops because I don't eat them anymore."

And the question of the day: *Having sex with someone is serious business, Sadie. Are you really ready to take that *next step* in your relationship with Brian?* I just stuffed pancakes in my mouth and looked at WS, who, God bless her (okay, there are times when I believe in Him), said, "Mom, how come you never had this talk with me about Slap?" She pretended to feel all left out and boo-hooey, and even dabbed at her eyes with a napkin. For about ten seconds I really liked her.

WS is on the pill, supposedly to help *lighten* her period, but that's how lots of girls end up on it. I won't even tell you how awful WS made the exam sound that you have to go through in order to get a prescription. Have I mentioned I have a very low tolerance for pain?

And so the *MOM sermon* continued o&o. Twenty minutes and three pancakes later, I heard about how you can get STDs whether you're on the pill or not, what it's like to be a pregnant teen, the true (i.e. grown-up) meaning of *intercourse* (barf-o-rama), and more.

I was so tired by the time we got home, I took a loooong nap with my Homer.

W3TP: Talking to your mother about sex.
Posted 10/17 at 9:34 PM

5 URock 3 ITalk

Sadie, i thot u were saving urself 4 ur tru luv, who u wud marry, that's wut u told me.
Posted 10/17 at 9:45 PM by sk8r4life

Um—Dustin, give it a rest—in Sadie's eyes u r no longer the best. My mom had the same talk with me, wonder if they write sumthin up just 4 parents. So if BB has a party while his mom is away, can I come 2? My big bro wud drive nd bring whatever booze u want. (He's the best!) Plz say yes!
Posted 10/17 at 10:30 PM by ems89

Of course she'll invite u, it wouldn't be a party without her two VBFs, rite!!!! It was gr8 to meet u, nd now I kno y Sadie luvs u so!!!! U shud definitely b a famous poet when u grow up—maybe my mom can help u.
Posted 10/17 at 10:32 PM by nujules4u

Monday, October 18
On Saturday night, when I was lying on the living-room floor in my sleeping bag between Jules and Emma, thinking about BB

and how much I love him already, all of a sudden I missed my dad. I wondered what he would say about BB, because sometimes he had some really good insights about Dustin. Unlike MOM, DAD doesn't ask a lot of questions or try to pry into my life, but he seemed to understand why I would adore a guy superglued to his skateboard.

I think BB is different, though. He is all about me, and vice versa. We already agreed we won't go out with anyone else. I know we're destined to be together because he is everything I want in a boy: strong, sexy, and not afraid to say what he thinks. I tried to tell DAD this on the phone last night but it wasn't the same as talking to him in person.

DAD has this idea that if he calls once a week, our relationship will be fine, but it's not the same. You can't see somebody's face long distance and know that their eyes are shining with love for you. WS says she *absolutely* will not go to see him over Thanksgiving break, but I have decided to go, even though it means flying on a plane all by myself. Lots of kids fly alone, some way younger than me. I'm not afraid of a terrorist or anything like that, but two things do bother me:

1. Getting off the plane and seeing my dad there with the woman who helped ruin my parents' marriage. Her name is Mabel. When I heard that, I knew it would be tough to be around her, because people who grow up with weird names have an extra challenge in life, imho.

2. Missing BB, who is so much a part of my life now I think I will die if I have to go five days without him! I gave up on getting a job because I want to spend every free minute with him, although MOM also said I shouldn't work during the school year, and it's all DAD's fault we don't have enough money, because he's not paying enough child support. This is an argument I could repeat by heart—she tells me every time we ring up at the grocery store what a tightwad DAD is, while he makes sure to let me know every time we talk that MOM gets regular child support checks and alimony from him. Ugh. It's just like a soap opera!

W3TP: Having to choose between two men you love too much.
Posted 10/18 at 10:09 PM

o URock o ITalk

Tuesday, October 19

Today I got another note from BB at school. It said:

Sadie:
I'm so glad you are my baby, life without you would make me crazy, so tell me you will always be my baby.
Your "BB"

Even though this was not really a poem, it felt like music was playing when I read it. I couldn't help giving him a big hug in the hallway. Just when that happened, Mia walked by and did one of those coughing *losers* sounds. Jules heard it and elbowed Mia, who tripped against the lockers. Then the two of them got into it again, luckily only verbal, but who knows what might have happened if Mr. Hammacker hadn't come running over to break it up?

<u>W3TP: Ever thinking you belonged with a skateboard slob who</u>
<u>never wrote you poems.</u>
Posted 10/19 at 4:05 PM

o URock 1 ITalk

I had a girlfriend I thought was great
Unfortunately, she didn't skate
Still, I thought she was first rate
And never guessed my heart she'd break

How's that for poetry?
Posted 10/19 at 4:45 PM by sk8r4life

Chapter Eight

Wednesday, October 20

My whole week has been consumed—and I mean <u>consumed</u>—
with planning this party that will *so* rock I can't stand it! After this
weekend I won't be a *new girl* anymore—I'll be part of a crowd.
Here are my resolutions:

1. Make some back-up friends, so if Jules is sick or whatever I
have someone to hang out with (although she and Emma will
always be my VBFs)

2. Be superfriendly at BB's party, so everyone will *die* to be my
friend

3. Have a sensational weekend with BB and grow even closer to
him

4. Dazzle BB beyond all imagination

5. Have too much fun with Emma and Jules

Once BB's mom leaves on Friday, which will be about 4 PMish,
I'll go over and help him get ready. We've already stockpiled
music, food, and booze (thanks to Emma's big brother). MOM

made me bring Jules home yesterday to confirm that we are spending part of the weekend together and that her sister will be there the entire time. (Both of these things are true, separately—thankfully she didn't ask more because I think she likes Jules and is desperate for me to make friends at my new school.)

After the party ends—which will be way late I'm sure, maybe even early the next morning—I'll still have BB all to myself for an entire day. Who knows what might happen?

W3TP: Making resolutions only on New Year's Eve.
Posted 10/20 at 6:23 PM

1 URock 1 ITalk

When things fall apart, don't say I didn't warn you. There's so much Brian isn't telling you. He has a problem, and if you listened to all the kids at school, you would realize this. I heard he punched in a window last year because he was mad at Mr. Hammacker. Think *anger management.*
Posted on 10/20 at 8:05 PM by kool2Bmia

Friday, October 22

The whole time I was talking to BB on the phone tonight, I wanted to ask him about what Mia posted the other day, even though I didn't really believe it, and everything is going so well with him I hate to make any problems. . . . Still, I finally asked in a cautious way about this rumor I had *heard.*

That was probably a mistake because he kept saying, "Who told you that?" and "Why does it matter to you?" But then finally, he said it was all because Mr. Hammacker (nose hairs) has always had it in for him. (Honestly, knowing Mr. Hammacker just a little, I could believe it. One day in class he made a girl do fifteen push-ups in front of everyone because she forgot her homework.)

Anyway, BB says Mr. Hammacker got on his case for talking in class, and it was a bad day anyway because it was right after his birthday and his dad hadn't shown up like he said he would (although he *didn't really care*), and something just snapped inside him. He <u>kicked</u> the door open, and it accidentally broke the window behind it.

Schools are so freaked out about violence these days. They actually brought drug dogs into my old school once, but they didn't find anything because even the dumbest kids wouldn't leave dope in their lockers—they'd be off somewhere dealing or smoking it. BB did get suspended for the incident with Mr. Hammacker, which seems totally unfair to me, but that's *zero tolerance* for you.

I told BB he should take a class in the martial arts, because he seems so interested in it, and they are supposed to help calm you down. He said he just likes to watch martial arts movies and read about them, and that as long as he has me, everything will be fine.

<u>W3TP: My new school's violence policy:</u>
<u>1. If a suspicious person enters the building, all the doors immediately lock, trapping everyone inside.</u>
<u>2. Students must go to assigned areas, where they are locked in and jammed together like those ducks at the carnival just sitting there waiting to be shot at.</u>

3. All the old and out-of-shape janitors and cafeteria workers are supposed to somehow come running and defend us from the dangerous person, but who knows how they'd do it (brooms and spatulas perhaps?).
Posted 10/22 at 1:23 AM

1 URock 1 ITalk

Even my grandma cud come up with a better disaster plan than that. I'm so xcited about the party, I don't kno how we'll make it through class all day!
Posted 10/22 at 6:45 AM by nujules4u

Sunday, October 24

OMG, I could never write about everything that happened at the party because it would take me forever. I can only say I've decided not to go visit DAD because I don't want to miss one second with BB. He is the strongest, cutest, funniest, nicest, most generous boy I have ever met in my life!

Things did get a little rowdy—one of the neighbors came over at 3 AM to complain. The guy threatened to call the police, which made BB so mad he nearly punched him. BB started yelling, "There are murderers and rapists out there, and you want the cops to come investigate innocent kids hanging out trying to have a little fun?" which was too funny and true, but the neighbor didn't think so. He got right in BB's face, and then me and BB's friend Ronzo had to hold BB back from punching the guy. We told the guy everyone was going home, and that's pretty much what happened after that.

BB was furious, but then he passed out, so me and Jules and Emma went for a walk, and then they fell asleep on the living-room floor. I went up to BB's room, of course. It was pure bliss to sleep in his arms and wake up with those beautiful, mysterious blue eyes looking deep into mine.

It didn't even matter that we had to clean everything up before his mom got home, and since BB didn't want to waste any booze, we (mostly he) drank what was left. The only real damage to the house was a hole in the wall near the front door, which I didn't remember seeing before, but BB laughed and said he kicked it after his neighbor left.

We weren't really sure how to fix the hole, but you can find any-thing online, so the four of us used some poster board and painted over it. It didn't look that great, but BB said his mom is so drunk most of the time, she won't even notice. So all in all, I spent most of the weekend with BB and my two VBF's—what could be better?

I had to leave before BB's mom came home, but he's already called me twice since then—tcfw. I think WS is jealous that I have such a great boyfriend.

W3TP: A mom who tells her son not to cause any trouble and then goes off to sleep with her (married) boyfriend. Then again, at least she didn't move to St. Louis to be with him.
Posted 10/24 at 7:55 PM

12 URock 6 ITalk

Damn, i new the party wud be mad fun, but it passed my

wildest dreams! Ronzo is sorta cute, dyt?
Posted 10/24 at 8 PM by nujules4u

Hey, itz me, Ronzo, ready 2 party hardy again. u rock, i'm so glad u came 2 our school. It wuz so fun when u and ur hot friend pre10ed 2 be the dumbass teachers we have. IM me soon, Jules!
Posted 10/24 at 8:30 PM by gr82h890

Even my big bro thot ur party was the end, and I'm still on the mend. when's the next 1? i'm glad 2 c u haven't changed Sades . . . luv u much!
Posted 10/24 at 9 PM by ems89

u hafta c the vid i made of Em dancin on the table. <u>take it off, baby, take it off</u>!
Posted 10/24 at 9:10 PM by rckzsohrd

netime u need booze, im da man. luv those bodacious babes, gimme, gimme! (xcept no comments about my lil sis's bod, man. . . .)
Posted 10/24 at 9:20 PM by 2muchfun

u bring the booze nd i will show u sum huge bangers. IM me now!
Posted 10/24 at 10 PM by babe4u

Thursday, October 28

Can you believe how many posts I got? And that was just the beginning—we all IMed for the next two hours, and although Jules has a BBF, who knows what might happen with her and

Ronzo? The party was the highlight of my year—if not my life!
But now here I am in Flex period and soooooo bored I can't do
any more work! My brain is dead, my body is tired, my heart
is heavy—in short, just another day in the life of a tenth
grader. . . . We have a sub today and she is pretty clueless, so
everyone in lab is posting like mad while she walks up and
down the aisles.

I must be bored desperate to do this, but Jules sent it:

Is it Luv?
<u>Underline</u> the ones that apply to you.

<u>I would do anything for him.</u>
<u>He's the first thing I think of when I wake.</u>
My parents adore him.
We have gone on vacation together.
<u>I know his favorite song.</u>
<u>He would never hurt me.</u>
He has bought me flowers.
<u>He would do anything for me. (?)</u>
We have gone through hardships together.
<u>We share many interests.</u>
<u>He is the most attractive guy I know.</u>
<u>He always makes me happy.</u>

Count up your underlines.
0–5: I don't think so. . . .
6–9: Go for it, girl!
10–11: You're on your way.
12: YES!

<u>W3TP: Meaningless online quizzes and girls like me who do them.</u>
Posted 10/28 at 11:13 AM

2 URock 2 ITalk

What a stupid quiz—only idiots take them. You need to move on!
Posted 10/28 at 11:15 AM by kool2Bmia

Malicious: miserable and mean, a person with evil intent. (As in Mia.)
Posted 10/28 at 11:20 AM by nujules4u

Chapter Nine

Friday, October 29

This is one of those days when I <u>really</u> despise my life (as opposed to the normal everyday feeling of just hating it). I thought the party would help me be at least a little popular—but the only people I like at my new school are still Jules and BB. Too bad I couldn't transport them and me back to my old school, where I at least liked some of the teachers and the school nurse.

After talking to some of the kids at BB's party who had dropped out of school or college, I started to think I should just drop out and work full time, and then I could buy a car and a cell phone and see BB whenever I want. I'm sure we could both get our GED right now—or at least he could because he gets such good grades already.

When I brought up the idea to BB, he looked right at me and said it was *stupid.* One word—but it really hurt my feelings, and he didn't even notice—in fact, he told Jules about it too. Because she truly is my VBF, she sided with me and said she felt the same way sometimes, especially since she has a semi-famous BBF who will soon make tons of $$. (Jules decided she just couldn't give him up for Ronzo.)

Ugh. Headache. I'm signing off.

W3TP: Making kids go to school until they're 16, whether they need to or not. Mr. Lowe says in the old days, kids used to do apprenticeships instead, where they learned on the job. mstm
Posted 10/29 at 6:33 PM

3 URock 3 ITalk

Itz not much fun here without u. mebbe we could have a party again? Guess wut? i found out Di is a cutter, her arms r a mess. now i feel bad 4 ever being mean 2 her. She nd Dustin rn't 2gether nemore either, but I think he is still nice to her.
Posted 10/29 at 7:05 PM by ems89

xcuse me, who sed u cud post sumthin so personal about me? nd i am not the worst in our school, there r lots of grls more xtreme than me.
Posted 10/29 at 7:10 PM by milhidi

Um hello, Emma—I don't even know you, but I can tell you need help and so does your friend Di. Cutting is a serious problem that can leave you with scars for the rest of your life and infections and other gross stuff. My mom told me all about it. There are many other (healthy) ways to express your stress.
Posted 10/29 at 7:15 PM by kool2Bmia

Saturday, October 30

Di, even though we're not friends, I need to tell you that I did a paper on cutting for Health class, and it is not good—not at all. (Here I am agreeing with Mia—can you believe it?) You're going to ruin your body forever, and then you'll be sorry, believe me. I found all these stories by girls who used to do it, and now they have terrible scars. My mom has some books you can look at if you want—or she will talk to you, I'm sure.

Emma, call Sadie back! Emma, call Sadie back! Better yet, come over and go trick-or-treating with me and BB (he he). His BF is having a party tomorrow that will rock.

W3TP: Girls who hurt, hurting themselves more.
Posted 10/30 at 10:02 PM

---

2 URock 1 ITalk

Yeah, but it won't b like the time when we went 2gether, dressed like 2 birds of a feather (that would b our *Mary-Kate and Ashley* year). Hafta figure sumthin new out 4 BB nd us!
Posted 10/31 at 2:02 AM by ems89

Sunday, October 31

In fourteen more hours I will wake up and get ready to go to school and see my sweet BB. I never tire of being with him! Emma just left a few minutes ago—MOM lets me go anyplace with her because Emma's mom is a psychologist at the hospital, which makes her a good influence on me.

At the Halloween party, BB came as Hercules, and me and Emma were his slave girls (think: Roman outfits with chains!)—it was too funny. He kept snapping his fingers and ordering us to do things for him like get him a beer or massage his shoulders (Emma wouldn't), but I thought it was hilarious. All the girls there were looking at him and wishing he was their BBF, I could tell, because his outfit showed how buff he is from working out every day. He really does have abs of steel.

BB kept picking me up and wouldn't put me down! Tomorrow he wants me to stay after school and lift weights with him, but I know WS will freak if I ask her to wait around. Too bad none of my friends can drive, but even if I could, MOM says she would never let me go somewhere alone with BB. For some reason (most likely WS's sabotage) she thinks he's *bad* for me. If she only knew how much I see him, she'd flip!

W3TP: People who can't take a joke and think your Halloween costume really means something about you.
Posted 10/31 at 4:22 PM

4 URock 4 ITalk

I don't care what you think, it is weird to pretend to be some-one's slave, especially when it sounds like you really are.
Posted 10/31 at 4:30 PM by kool2Bmia

Envy: a quality displayed by an individual who covets a belonging or quality of another person. Can't people take a joke? I wuzn't even there becuz I had 2 babysit, but it sounds like a total hoot.
Posted 10/31 at 4:45 PM by nujules4u

Hey, itz me Ronzo, and i thought Emma wuz 2 hot. IM me, babe. . . . . .
Posted 10/31 at 6 PM by gr82h890

Playah alert! Playah alert! Beware of Ronzo the Big Bad Playah. . . .
Posted 10/31 at 6:30 PM by nujules4u

Chapter Ten

Monday, November 1

Tonight the doorbell rang, and when I answered it I almost fell over because there was DAD. He grabbed me and hugged me so hard I started to cry, and I think he had tears in his eyes, even though he pretended not to.

Slap and WS were watching TV, but when Slap saw who it was he jumped up and hugged DAD because they hung out a lot when DAD still lived with us. (Slap's dad died of cancer last year, so I think DAD was sort of a substitute father for him.)

WS got really upset and threw the remote at both of them and stomped upstairs. DAD said he had a chance to come back on a business trip and wanted to see all of us, so he did. But guess what? I am the only one who would go out to dinner with him. MOM was about to say I couldn't because she was so mad at him for just coming over, but then she said okay. I think she wants him to talk to me about BB because I won't answer her when she tries to get all chummy and find out how I feel about him.

So DAD asked a million questions, but not only about me. He wanted to know how WS was doing, and even how MOM and Slap and Aunt Sara were doing. He is staying at a hotel till Thursday, so I asked if he wanted to meet BB and Jules tomorrow night, and he said of course; he wouldn't miss it. That's good, because I have a feeling no one else in our house is going to want to spend any time with him.

When I got home and went upstairs, WS was in bed with the covers over her head and wouldn't speak to me.

W3TP: Your DAD being a visitor in your life, and not even a welcome one. How can people be unhappy to see someone they love?
Posted 11/1 at 11:37 PM

o URock o ITalk

Thursday, November 4
Give URocks! Need URocks! Will take URocks in exchange for food!

Last night, me and DAD and BB went out for Chinese and spent about three hours talking, and it turns out my DAD is taking karate lessons and planning to buy a motorcycle—real guy-bonding topics. BB thinks DAD is the greatest. Jules had to work and couldn't come with us, so I did a lot of listening to boring guy things. It was only bearable because of a lot of under-the-table handholding.

I could tell BB sort of missed his dad after being with mine because later on the phone he went into that whole *it doesn't matter* bit about not seeing his dad again, just like WS says *there's nothing wrong with goths* at least once a day. When someone goes o&o about something, it is important, I've learned.

It's funny how you can get used to not seeing someone, but when you see them the missing starts all over again, just as bad. When he came to say good-bye this morning before going back to St. Louis, it was like hearing the news that he and MOM were splitting up all over again. It gave me such a bad headache at school, I ended up at Ms. Penders's office and then got to go home early because WS has a free period at the end of the day. She and I totally vegged out and watched every old sitcom on the Home channel until MOM arrived with pizza for supper.

DAD pretty much reconvinced me to come for Thanksgiving too.

W3TP: Four days (96 hours) seems like an eternity to be away from my BB.
Posted 11/4 at 10:34 PM

28 URock 2 ITalk

i can tolly relate, itz just 2 damn hard 2 b away from those u love. my BBF is pissed becuz my mom nd dad sed i cudn't come to NYC 4 T-day becuz they won't b there. a/i it's my problem they want to spend the holidays in Switzerland!!!!!! w3tp?
Posted 11/4 at 10:35 PM by nujules4u

Your father is with you even when he is far away. He is a caring and kind man underneath it all, even if he did screw his family

over. People make mistakes. It will all work out for you and your sister, imho.
Posted 11/4 at 11:16 PM by gr82bgoth

Friday, November 5

This morning I could barely drag myself out of bed—it's been that way all week for some reason, but tomorrow MOM and WS are going to visit colleges again, so Aunt Sara is *babysitting* me . . . YAHOO! I can stay out as late as I want because she is a pushover and also falls asleep really early and won't even know if I'm home or not.

BB and I have big plans, but it all depends on whether his mom is around or not. Unlike my MOM, she doesn't do the drill sergeant routine and try to hear every detail of BB's day, but if she knew what went on, she would be upset. BB says she was so busy talking on her cell phone and checking her email when she got home last time, she never noticed the hole in the wall that we fixed. My MOM would have been all over that in a heartbeat.

W3TP: Feeling so excited about deceiving a relative you care about.
Posted 11/5 at 11:16 PM

4 URock o ITalk

Tuesday, November 9

BB's mom totally left for the weekend, g/f, so it was just the two of us. I snuck back into my house in the mornings, so Aunt Sara · thought I slept there all night. Thankfully Homer saw me right away and didn't bark.

Here are some more things I've learned (and love) about my sweetest, dearest, kindest BB:

☺ He wants to be a veterinarian (he is so sweet with Homer, who recognizes him now). I could see us working together in our own animal clinic.

☺ He thinks WS should treat me nicer, but says Slap is okay and my DAD is the greatest.

☺ His favorite food is cookies—any kind. He can eat a whole package of Oreos and not feel full.

No wonder I love BB more than I will ever love any other boy in my life. Jules says we look so happy together, it even makes her jealous.

Our only problem is we can't blog or talk online. I found out that even if he wanted to, he couldn't because he broke his computer when he threw the monitor after seeing posts from Dustin on my site! I know it's a bit much, but isn't that romantic? His mom has lots of money, but she won't buy him another one because it's actually the second time he did it. (The first time was when his dad found something he posted and told his mom to take it away.) Luckily he has a cell phone and can call me any time he wants, as long as I make sure to keep our phone by my bed and answer it before WS wakes up.

W3TP: Nothing! Everything is right, right, right!
Posted 11/9 at 6:15 PM

10 URock 0 ITalk

Friday, November 12

My new school sucks even more than I thought possible. Today
BB got suspended for two weeks just because he used the F-word
to Mr. Hammacker (nose hairs), who is BB's worst enemy and
always will be. They were especially hard on him because of what
happened last year. I don't think I've ever seen BB so mad. He
kicked his locker (no one else saw), and then while he was
waiting outside to be picked up, he used every swear word I
could think of. When I tried to hug him he pushed me away and
I tripped on the curb and fell.

He was instantly sorry and apologized about a hundred times,
but all I could do was go home and crawl in my bed with
Homer. Later, BB called and said his mom grounded him from
<u>everything</u> when she found out what happened at school—
even talking on the phone. She also called his dad and they
decided to hire some college guy to *supervise* BB because
things need to change. (So much for that—he already called
me twice on a prepaid cell phone one of his friends let him
borrow.)

<u>W3TP: When adults start taking over your life and changing things that don't need changing.</u>
Posted 11/12 at 3:30 PM

25 URock 7 ITalk

Um, Clueless, I happened to be there, along with 20 other kids,
when the whole thing went down. Your precious BBF didn't just
"use" the F-word, he screamed it AND he got right in Mr.
Hammacker's face and hit the desk with his fist when he did it.
I thought for sure BB was going to punch him. <u>You should find</u>

<u>a new boyfriend.</u>
Posted 11/12 at 4:30 PM by kool2Bmia

i saw it 2, nd altho i don't rilly post much, u need 2 kno that ur
BF is lying 2 u. guys tell girlz wut they want 2 hear all the time, nd
we believe it. Mr. H is a jerk, but it wuz scary how mad ur BF got
about a little thing.
Posted 11/12 at 4:35 PM by hshoney90

itz not fair 2 write things about sumone who can't defend himself
becuz he doesn't believe in posting his every thought online.
every1 knos Mr. H is a big homo nd has a crush on BB. . . .
Posted 11/12 at 4:45 PM by gr82h890

So you're saying BB is a homophobe? Or there's something
wrong with a teacher being gay? People like you really need to
raise your awareness of GLBT issues, which are no joke and not
something to pretend you know about when you don't. I had Mr.
H last year, and believe me, he is not gay, unless getting caught
cheating on your wife with our beloved and very female 9th grade
guidance counselor is "gay."
Posted 11/12 at 4:50 PM by imogaynsoru

itz not ok 2 b gay, itz a sin, but that's bside the point. Mr. H getz
2 hyper nd wants all the babes 2 think he iz macho. when i had
him he did sumthin similar 2 me nd i got kicked out of skool 4 a
week. stand by ur man, nugrl!
Posted 11/12 at 5 PM by gld4grlz

gld4grlz, I graduated with you and believe me, you were going
nowhere anyway. It didn't take Mr. H to screw you up. All of my
high school buds and I got a big laugh out of your post because

we remember what a loser you were.
Posted 11/12 at 6 PM by colegstud84

Sadie, wuzzup? We haven't talked in 4evah—r u okay? IM me nd let me know how u r. Sorry if I caused problems 4 u nd ur nu BBF.
Posted 11/12 at 6:19 PM by sk8r4life

Chapter Eleven

Wednesday, November 17

There are so many rumors at school about BB, I can't stand it. Every day it's a major challenge to drag myself out of bed, get in the car, and go back to school.

If I didn't have Jules, I think I would just skip every day until I got kicked out too. I couldn't even post because I was so upset, and yes, I even resorted to visiting the evil Ms. Penders to get away from it all. But now is the time when BB and me usually talk on the phone and, of course, he is still grounded. I am desperate. (His mom caught him talking to me on the borrowed cell phone, and, judging from the screaming I heard before we got cut off, we won't be in touch for a long time. Can you believe she accused him of stealing it?)

Slap overheard me telling Homer all this and tried to console me in his uniquely goth way. He told me life is like a river, with many twists and turns, and when you hit the rapids you need a copilot or a really safe raft. Maybe he is right; maybe we lack meaning in our lives and look to others for it. That's *profound,* as Ms. Gardner, my English teacher, would say, and I wonder if I can use it for my paper on "A Person Who Changed My Life." Slap would be thrilled, especially if I included a pic of him. Then again, who but me and WS would appreciate a tall skinny guy with shoulder-length black hair, wearing a black shirt, black pants, and black shoes? He and BB are complete opposites—just like WS and me.

W3TP: Everything, suddenly.
Posted 11/17 at 7 PM

14 URock o ITalk

Friday, November 19

Today I got an *anonymous* note in math that said BB was being sent to reform school by his dad. I couldn't figure out who sent it because when I looked around it seemed like everyone was laughing at me in that sneaky way teachers don't see.

brb. . . .

I just tried to call BB on his regular phone, but his *guard* Ryan told me he wasn't allowed to talk to me or anyone else. I only hope BB will somehow get his hands on a cell phone, or even better, break out and come see me. Hmm . . . I wonder if Jules and me could sneak over there.

W3TP: Being grounded from seeing someone who is good for you AND punishing two people instead of just one. Parents should think about how their actions affect everyone else.
Posted 11/19 at 7:13 PM

6 URock 2 ITalk

Sades, come over nd c me!
Posted 11/19 at 7:30 PM by nujules4u

hey u, don't b blue. want me to visit u?
Posted 11/19 at 8 PM by ems89

Monday, November 22

No word from BB, and I feel like my heart is breaking. WS actually drove me to his house, and for one minute I thought I was brave enough to go up and peek in a window, but then Ryan (I assume that's who it was) came out to get the newspaper and I totally freaked. WS floored it and we screeched out of there so fast I thought the car would have major damage. (It didn't.)

Aunt Sara came over tonight after MOM told her I was moping all weekend, but I couldn't talk to her, even when she and I went out for pizza. She asked me all these questions that I could tell were designed to get me talking, but it didn't work. Finally she just gave up and we ate in silence, which wasn't much fun, either. I spent the rest of the night lying on my bed with Homer and feeling miserable.

Now it looks like I <u>have</u> to go to St. Louis for Thanksgiving, because my DAD bought the ticket and made me feel guilty and then downright mad when I told him I wasn't sure I could come out there. Have I <u>ever once</u> made him feel guilty for all the stuff he's done? The answer would be no, of course.

Jules is so sweet. She tries to cheer me up with random pictures, like this one of me and Emma.

W3TP: Don't adults realize they need to make things easier for us, not harder?
Posted 11/22 at 8:25 PM

4 URock 2 ITalk

Yeah I kno xactly how u feel! it is tuff sumtimes 2 keep going nd enjoy life when everything is falling apart nd the ppl u luv r far away nd don't even call or write u.
Posted 11/22 at 8:30 PM
by nujules4u

u 2 r so depressing! i wish i had some magic cure 2 make u happy. if we cud just hang out, maybe it wud help? Call me!
Posted 11/22 at 8:45 PM by ems89

Wednesday, November 24

Here I am in St. Louis with my DAD and yes, Mabel, who is so pretty she could be on television, was there too. She is trying to make me her friend, but I'm just giving her the silent treatment. DAD came in the bedroom before I went to sleep and said I should be nicer to her. w/e.

I am seriously depressed and can't sleep because:

1. I didn't get to see BB before I flew out here. Whoever Ryan is, I probably wouldn't want to tangle with him—but isn't it illegal to treat your kid like that? I asked Jules if I should maybe report BB's mom to the police for abuse, and she said OMG, NO! So I won't.

2. Both WS and MOM are upset with me for spending T-Day with DAD. In fact, Slap drove me to the airport to save me and them a lot of bad and mad feelings. I've gotten closer to Slap lately; he might be as good a listener as BB. Plus, in his own gothic way, he loves WS as much as BB loves me.

3. Everyone except Jules hates me. I can't figure out why, because I haven't done anything to anyone, but Jules says I'm guilty by association, and all anyone at our school cares about is having the right things on their record when they apply for college.

4. Mabel thinks she's my new best friend and wants to do all kinds of stupid stuff together like go jogging (a/i!) and bake cookies and talk about DAD.

Double W3TP: Being expected to become best buds with your DAD's girlfriend.
Posted 11/24 at 10:30 PM

2 URock o ITalk

Thursday, November 25
pos . . . brb

Jules is the best! She sent me this to cheer me up, so here goes.

You need a piece of paper to do it, but it's fun.

Write:
♥ The name of someone of the opposite sex.
♥ Which of the following colors you like most: pink, brown, purple, aqua, or orange.
♥ The first initial of your last name.
♥ Which month you were born.
♥ One hope you have for the future.

Once you're done, scroll down to find out what life holds for you!

....
....
....
....
....
....
....
....
....
....

1. You are absolutely bonkers about this person.

2. If you picked the color:

Pink: You are cheerful and your life is full of joy.

Brown: You are reserved but sometimes aggressive.

Purple: You have a calm soul and aren't easily upset.

Aqua: You are a spur-of-the-moment person who is very affectionate to those you care about.

Orange: You try to be happy but sometimes need others to perk you up.

3. If your initial is:

A–K: You have many friends and admirers.

L–R: You live life to the fullest and will enjoy great success.

S–Z: You enjoy helping others and will accomplish many good
deeds.

4. If you were born in:

January–March: Your sweet romance will fade, but you will
remember it always.

April–June: The coming year will be a good one for you and your
true love.

July–September: This year will be one of great growth and
excitement for you and your sweetie.

October–December: This year will be a rocky one but will pave the
way to future passion.

5. Whatever you wrote will come true only if you send this quiz to
ten friends within one hour of finishing it.

My answers:

1. Guess who

2. Orange

3. M

4. March

5. Many happy times with BB and my friends

W3TP: Thanksgiving dinner with Mabel. For the first time ever, I didn't even eat everything on my plate, let alone ask for seconds.
Posted 11/25 at 6:12 PM

o URock 1 ITalk

Sades, since u can't IM from ur dad's, i'll write a long note 2
cheer u up! i miss my mom nd dad today, they r both in Europe,
can u believe it? in fact, i'm a *little* pissed they would do that
when i haven't seen them in so long! Mona sez we just have 2 be

happy 2gether. she isn't a very good cook, so our dinner was not the best either, but she tries. . . .

HOWEVER, this AM there was a knock on the door nd who do u think wuz there? my o&o BBF!!! he drove all the way from NYC in his nu car, a BMW convertible, series 7. we hugged 4ever! 2 bad u can't meet him as he has 2 go back 2morrow be4 u get home.
Posted 11/25 at 8 PM by nujules4u

Chapter Twelve

Sunday, November 28

Well, I'm back home, where no one hangs over my shoulder every time I turn the computer on. (DAD's is in the dining room, so it was touch and go to post at all. Luckily, Mabel distracted him every now and then.)

The plane ride home was so boring I managed to do my entire English assignment in my head. Maybe my student teacher last year was right about me being a good writer—sometimes ideas for stories just come to me.

How I Spent My Thanksgiving Vacation

This Thanksgiving was an unusual one for me because I spent it with a complete stranger. The only other person I knew was my father, but he is kind of a stranger to me since he and my mother separated this summer and he moved to St. Louis. St. Louis is the gateway to the West, but for my father it has been the gateway to a new life.

When you are a kid, you assume your parents will always be the same Mom and Dad you grew up with, and that's one thing you can count on for better or worse. It's quite a shock to discover that one of them is not at all the person you believed him or her to be. This is the experience I had with my father.

Although he's been away from us for only three months, he grew his hair long and pierced his ear. He is no longer the straight-edge daddy I looked up to as a little girl. The apartment where he lives now has all the things he would never buy us: a big-screen TV, brand-new computer, and, believe it or not, a PlayStation. Yes, my forty-six-year-old father has begun to play Grand Theft Auto, and even taught me how. He seems happy, but sort of like Christmas Day happy, when you are overwhelmed with new things but know that the next day you will go back to your unexciting life and have nothing to look forward to.

In addition to this, a new woman has stepped into the role my mother used to play, at least partially. She is closer to my age than she is to his, which might be why he is acting so different. His new girlfriend, Mabel, seems to be a little unstable, however. One night she came in (uninvited) and sat on the bed I was sleeping in and told me her life story. She has been in the hospital for depression two times and switched jobs four times in the last year. Currently, she works "in retail," which means Walmart. There seems to be too much of Mabel, just like there was too much food on the table at Thanksgiving. She has spun-gold red hair that hangs all around her face in big curls. Her skin looks like white velvet, and although we never touched, I expect that if we did, I would sink right into her like a big pillow. She is as tall as my dad and has curves everywhere, even on her elbows.

My mother is the exact opposite of Mabel. She is short with frizzy brown hair that she tucks behind her ears, and she would never leave a job, even if she really hated it and came home stressed every night.

So you might say this Thanksgiving filled me with many surprises. Sure, Mabel made the traditional turkey and pumpkin pie and talked about the weather and sports and all the other family members who weren't there, just like we might at home. Afterward, I felt stuffed; not with food, but with all the discoveries I had made during my family holiday.

Not sure if there should be a semicolon in that last sentence, but I think this is a pretty good essay, if I do say so myself.

When MOM picked me up at the airport this afternoon, she was tight-lipped like she gets when she wants to yell at me or say something rude but is trying to hold it back. Finally I asked her how Thanksgiving went, and she did what I do when I'm mad and don't want to talk: "Fine." How was Aunt Sara's turkey? "Fine." So I gave up and sat in silence until we got home, where my dear doggie covered me with licks and kisses. (To be honest, he does the same exact thing every day when I come home from school.)

WS didn't even come down from our room to say hi. When I went up to unpack and tried to be nice, she gave the same answers MOM did: "Fine," "Okay," and the ever-famous "Yup."

Just about the time I felt sort of sorry to be back home, MOM burst into the room crying and said she missed me like crazy and

Thanksgiving wasn't the same without me there. She even said WS missed me.

Of course, WS shouted, "AS IF!"

MOM hugged me as hard as she could, which made me cry too, but WS just got huffy and slammed her book shut in a real obvious way and said she couldn't be around two women with PMS at the same time. Next thing you know MOM ordered pizza and we all sat on the bedroom floor, and they asked me a million questions about DAD and Mabel. WS said I made Mabel sound like a parade float, and we laughed and laughed, even though it wasn't that funny.

But, there's still no word from BB 😞 (sound of ♥ breaking in background). Jules hasn't heard anything, either. So I have to wait for tomorrow, when we will finally be reunited in school!

W3TP: Thanksgiving should be a happy time.
Posted 11/28 at 11:34 PM

2 URock o ITalk

Monday, November 29
Oh bliss. Finally my dearest, most adorable, charming, and beloved BB and I were reunited! At our lockers we saw each other and ran together and held on for dear life until one of the teachers (guess who?) told us to knock it off. For the first time ever, I skipped out of school to be with him for the afternoon, but we had to use a secret exit Jules found (my lips are sealed). I also had to get to the answering machine first when I got home so I could delete the

message telling MOM I was absent from my afternoon classes.

So here's the story: BB has been under virtual lock and key for the last month, after his dad showed up and threatened to send him to boot camp. This guy Ryan is supposed to supervise BB every minute he's not in school, and I guess he's in cop training at college and that's how BB's dad knew him. There are lots of strict rules now, like no TV, phone, or computer at all, no going anywhere without Ryan after school or on the weekends, and no friends (me included) at the house. (I guess his dad noticed the hole in the wall and talked to the neighbor guy about the party incident too.)

BB is so mad at his dad, he called him a bunch of bad names and said he didn't know why his dad couldn't stay out of his life, or else come back and be a real father. Part of that I could understand, because of my situation.

But there's only one way to describe how BB feels about his worst enemy of all, Mr. Hammacker: <u>hate</u>. He told me he passed Mr. H in the hallway this morning and Mr. H gave him the finger (but pretended he was scratching his ear). BB went o&o about Mr. H until I couldn't stand it anymore, so I put my arms around him and started kissing him. But it didn't really help him be less angry.

We went to the park and he kept doing dumb things like kicking trees and swearing and throwing stones in the pond. I wished Homer was there to distract him because I sure couldn't, which made me feel invisible, like I didn't even matter. Then, suddenly, he cheered up when I asked about the online game he and Ronzo are creating—where kids bring weapons to school or karate chop teachers they don't like. Of course, since he has no access to the computer, that project is on hold.

"Except for you, my life sucks, Sadie," he told me, and there were tears in his eyes. Then he hugged me and I told him WS's motto: "Life sucks and then you die," but that I couldn't accept that.

We kissed for a while and I could feel the tension flow out of him, but by then I had to leave. What happened next was so romantic: he took off his gold-chain necklace and put it on me and made me promise to wear it forever. He said his dad got it for him when he turned 13 and he hasn't taken it off since—until now.

When WS saw me coming toward the car with him, she got this dark look on her face under her white makeup and told me to "GET IN RIGHT NOW." In the car, she really lost it and started yelling at me that I should have some self-respect and dump BB because he's nothing but trouble.

"Don't you hear what everyone says about him, Sadie? How can you ignore that?"

"Oh yeah, well how about the things everyone at our old school used to say about your beloved Slap?" I snapped back. If I were the kind of person to fight physically, I would have punched her in the face right about then.

Then something awful happened. WS grabbed my arm real hard and told me that one of her *friends* at our new school heard I was going out with BB and told WS that BB beat up another kid real bad last summer when he was visiting his dad. Since it didn't happen at our school, his dad used his cop connections to hush everything up and BB got off. I don't know which hurt more, her fingers digging into me or her words. Plus, I was really scared because she didn't stop the car to tell me all this.

When we got home, I took Homer for a long walk and told him the entire story because he is really the best listener I know. Hearing myself talk about it all, I knew WS was just jealous because she has never fit in like I have. At least that was true at my old school. Who knows now?

W3TP: Knowing that someone is kind and gentle, but having other people think he isn't.
Posted 11/29 at 9:18 PM

6 URock 4 ITalk

Sadie, you need a major reality check. You have been in a
perpetual state of denial ever since we met. It's not that no one
likes you; it's the people you hang around with that are causing
you trouble. Your sister may be weird, but you should listen
to her.
Posted 11/29 at 10:10 PM by kool2Bmia

Witch: a shrewish woman of evil intent, sometimes with magical
powers. Might I add, someone who meddles in everyone else's
life even though she should just take the hint to myob!!! Mia, if u
ever went to my old school in NYC, u would b so dead by now!!!
Posted 11/29 at 10:20 PM by nujules4u

Sades, i'm worried about u. IM me plz!
Posted 11/29 at 10:30 PM by sk8r4life

What your sister told you is true.
Posted on 11/29 at 10:35 PM by uduntknome

Chapter Thirteen

Wednesday, December 1

After my fight with WS, I was so upset I went to bed and skipped supper, which means I got a terrible headache during French class the next day at school. The wicked nurse of the west acts like it's her own personal bed you're asking to lie down on, but she has seen me so many times in the last two days, she finally called MOM and told her I needed to go home.

Jules told me true love always triumphs, but those posts about BB really bother me. No one knows the kind and caring side of BB like I do. For example, he wrote me another poem:

Sadie, special lady,
Our time together has been tuff
But when I'm with you, I can't get enough
Believe in me and I'll make you glad
Even if we must pass through a time that's sad
No one understands how sweet you are
At nighttime I look up and you're the brightest star

Be strong and don't give up on our love
Our destiny to be together comes from above

Isn't he amazing? I don't know any other girl whose BBF writes such beautiful poetry to her. It makes me determined to prove everyone wrong.

Of course, after Poisonous Penders called, MOM came to pick me up and I could instantly tell she was upset. She started talking, talking, talking, all about how the doctor says my headaches are *psychosomatic* (i.e. imaginary). I told her I saw a TV show where a girl had a brain tumor and they told her the same thing. After about twenty minutes, I began to regret going down to Ms. Penders and decided I will never, ever do it again, even if my head feels like it's about to explode.

Then I got even sorrier because MOM pulled the car over and started crying—the ultimate hand grenade of parenting. It didn't matter that I got an A and the comment "Excellent, Sadie!" on my paper about Thanksgiving vacation. That just made her cry harder, because after she read it she said it showed how dysfunctional our family is. (She should have heard the other kids' papers. One kid wrote about his mom finally going into rehab for coke addiction and another one wrote about being worried her dad was going to go to jail for insurance fraud.)

Anyway, we were jammed in the front seat, and MOM kept on hugging me and crying and talking at the same time. She told me, "I'm trying so hard, Sadie, so hard. Every day at work I wish I could quit and stay home and play piano like I used to, but that's not going to happen. All day long I listen to people's problems, but I should be home, listening to yours."

Did I mention that my MOM plays the piano majorly well? And that when she had kids, she quit her job at a counseling center and got some gigs playing music? It was nice because almost every day when I came home from school, she'd be playing the piano, a baby grand that my dad bought her for her birthday one year. Now it's crammed into our living room with unpacked boxes sitting on top of it.

So finally, when I was ready to pull my hair out piece by piece because I was so frustrated, I told her that going to the nurse wasn't about her or DAD or the divorce, but about BB and the trouble he was in and that no one understands that he has turned over a new leaf. Then to my surprise I started crying too, because I could hear in my words how deeply I love him.

After I didn't have any tears left, I felt like you do when you finish barfing: it's better—sometimes even excellent—because you got rid of what was bothering you. (btw, this is my theory of bulimia too, but in a sort of symbolic way. If I ever become a psychologist instead of a writer, I will do a study on it.)

At first, I thought my MOM felt better too, but then a thunder-cloud passed over her face as she realized the answers to all her questions related to BB. She demanded to know if he had been arrested—EVER—how often I saw him, did we have sex, was I ever at his house alone with him, and so on. It was tafw. I put on what Slap calls a *neutral face* (to be used with any authority figure you can't just blow off) and didn't answer any of her questions. This only made her angrier, but at least she wasn't crying.

By the time we got home, WS was home too, all huffed up because the office told her I left school sick after she waited around to drive me home. It was like two MOMs yelling at me, because she started in about BB again too.

Homer got so excited by the yelling he barked and barked and jumped up on me with his paws on my shoulders (which is bad behavior; I saw a TV show that said it is the dog equivalent of a little kid throwing a tantrum for attention). I let MOM and WS yell and put him on his leash and went for a long walk because the drama was way too much for me.

Now my MOM (with WS's help, I'm sure) is going to make it even harder for me to see BB. It all goes back to Poisonous Penders, who could have solved everything by simply letting me hang out and maybe even asking in a nice way what was going on, like Ms. Armstrong used to do. In fact, it's thanks to Ms. Armstrong that I even started my blog and it does help, despite the fact that I'm constantly distracted, thinking about what to say (or not) online. And although I never get enough URocks, the ITalks are GREAT (most times)!

W3TP: Why is it so much worse when your mom cries than when she yells?
Posted 12/1 at 10:56 PM

20 URock 6 ITalk

Hang in there, superchick, don't let this get u sic. Soon it will b Xmas nd i got u an awesome present. Member last yr when u nd me got each other tie-dye tights that were 2 cool nd wore them 2 school the day after break? ur still my VBF 4 life nd i'm here 4 u. call or IM me soon!
Posted 12/1 at 11:03 PM by ems89

i wondered wut happened 2 u!!! ur mom is just being a mom, that's how they r. my mom does the same thing whenever we talk on the phone, i can hardly stand it sumtimes!!! but Emma is rite, soon we have time off nd maybe all 3 of us can get 2gether and go 2 the mall or a movie. nd guess what, my sis nd Abby may be oot on New Year's. . . . u kno wut that means! Party, Party, Party!
Posted 12/1 at 11:10 PM by nujules4u

Listen, you sound like a nice-enough girl, let me tell you that Brian Boynes is bad news. I don't go to your school, but I met him at a party and we went out for about three months, until I realized he has a major drinking problem. (Has he told you he gets drunk _every_ night in his bedroom?) He only hit me one time, but it was pretty hard and my parents saw the bruise and said, "That's it." They called his mom but she didn't do anything.

After we broke up, I went away to private school because I was afraid to be around him anymore. And btw, Mr. H actually looks a little bit like his father, if you've ever seen him.
Posted 12/1 at 11:15 PM by uduntknome

i think it's romantic, like Romeo nd Juliet.
Posted 12/1 at 11:20 PM by nujules4u

I think you're a colossal idiot. Getting hit is never romantic. The statistics on domestic violence are appalling, and my father says it is harder and harder to prosecute because women (like you) think it's okay.
Posted 12/1 at 11:30 PM by kool2Bmia

hey, if he eva hurtz u in anyway, let me kno. i don't believe in

violence, but i will majorly *talk* 2 that dude.
Posted 12/1 at 11:45 PM by sk8r4life

Friday, December 3

No matter what anyone says, you can't change your heart—not
that I'd even want to stop loving BB. He has made mistakes just
like everyone else in this world, but people deserve second
chances.

It's the same as with my DAD, who did some rotten things to us,
but I still love him. Incidentally, he's coming here for Xmas!
MOM and Aunt Sara are taking a cruise on the 26th, so DAD will
be staying for a whole week. Wa-hoo! Wonder if Mabel will come?
MOM—and maybe WS—would kill him if that happened.

Why does everything have to be so complicated?

W3TP: My entire life.
Posted 12/3 at 11:12 PM

o URock 1 ITalk

hey u, here's wut 2 do: b a superchick! use ur superpower nd talk
2 BB about how u feel.
Posted 12/3 at 11:53 PM by ems89

Chapter Fourteen

Tuesday, December 14

BB told me we have to be really careful about skipping school
(which we've been doing a lot lately), and when I got my midterm
report, I knew he was right. MOM and DAD <u>flipped</u> when they
saw my grades (or heard about them, in DAD's case). At first I
thought about forging MOM's signature, but WS brought her
straight-A version home at the same time, so that was impossible.
DAD, who is generally a pushover, said he could understand a
few *digressions* if at least some of my grades were good, but
except for English, they're not. And he still got on me for missing
afternoon classes, even after I blamed it on my headaches.
MOM, of course, had four words: "You are so grounded." It's
amazing—after all their fighting, they are both in total agreement
about what a disappointment I am and how desperately I need to
change my ways.

Luckily, my MOM's boss, who apparently works psycho-miracles
over at the hospital, said it's not a good idea to restrict me from
seeing BB—but we should be together only under *controlled*

circumstances. If they think we'll sit on the sofa with them watching home videos, they are so wrong. Aunt Sara, my only ally, said she got straight Fs on her report card one time and look what a success she is now, but MOM just gave her a dirty look.

"Creative types," Aunt Sara says, "have to be given space during their formative years." But she didn't jump at the idea when MOM asked if she wanted to trade places with her.

For the first time in my life, I've seriously thought about running away—with BB, that is. I know we could make it on our own. Besides, what do I have here but my few (though incredible) friends who will be there for me no matter where I go?

BB says we just have to play it straight until all this blows over. It's hard, though, because every morning when Mr. Hammacker— the supposedly mature adult—walks by us, he has a malicious look on his face (honest to God, it's pure evil, "I'm gonna getcha one way or the other and no one will ever know"), focused right at BB and me. Then BB's arm muscles tense up and his face looks nothing like the gentle person's I know, who strokes my hair when I cry.

Since BB didn't take me up on the martial arts idea, I found another solution for his need to *express emotions appropriately*: I checked out a book from the library on anger problems and read the whole thing. It said that sometimes after a divorce, a kid is mad at his or her parents but can't tell them that, so they find someone else to take it out on. (This would explain why WS is so rotten to me most of the time.) imho, this is BB's whole problem with Mr. Hammacker, who must remind him of his dad in some ways.

I got some index cards, decorated them with hearts and kisses, and wrote down a few of the book's ideas so BB could use them during moments of stress. Some of them were pretty lame: *Count to ten*, *Take a deep breath*, and so on, but one made a lot of sense: *Talk to someone who cares about you*. (That would be me.)

I gave BB the cards in school today. He told me I am *too sweet* and checked to make sure I was still wearing the necklace he gave me. As if I would take it off! (But I do hide it under my shirt to avoid annoying MOM questions.)

Now I have to think about something to do for Jules, because her parents are *traveling* during Xmas vacation and she won't even get to see them. That's just wrong.

W3TP: Parents who are rich and happily married but who don't spend time with their daughter because they would rather be famous. (Sorry, Jules, but it sucks, imho.)
Posted 12/14 at 8:19 PM

---

6 URock 3 ITalk

u r amazing. sumday u will b a gr8 psychologist or sumthin. u always were helpful 2 other ppl—that's the Christian way. i kno u have anuthr BBF now, but maybe we can chill sum over Xmas, like old times.
Posted 12/14 at 8:25 PM by sk8r4lifeM

u can't say that about my mom nd dad, cuz they rilly do luv me. they promised I wud b amazed by the special present they r sending, nd i get to go with them 2 Hawaii on spring break.
Posted 12/14 at 8:45 PM by nujules4u

Please forgive me, Jules! I meant it in a good way and, of course, your parents are great—I'm jealous!
Posted 12/14 at 9 PM by nugrl90

Thursday, December 16

Today after English Ms. Gardner asked if I would be interested in working on the school paper. At first I hadn't liked her much because she is so short, and who wants a teacher on your own eye level? But she said she's been really impressed by my writing, so I told her maybe I would try it. I admit: in the back of my mind were the suck-up points I would get from MOM and DAD if I do it. And who knows, if psychology isn't for me (which seems likely now that I've read that anger book), maybe I can write something that will hit the best-seller list, and they'll realize Aunt Sara was right about me.

Jules and I (see, proper grammar and everything!) went to the mall Xmas shopping today, but she only looked, because why buy presents here when she can get them in Manhattan, where everything is better? I got BB the coolest wristband. It's leather and snaps together and I got letters (my initials, of course) carved into it. It's brown because he wears brown boots to school almost every day, so I think it will look good and also remind him of me ☺.

Jules says we can have a small party at her house on New Year's since her sister will be visiting Abby's dad. We spent the rest of the evening at the park, talking about who to invite and how Mona can call up my parents and tell them I'm staying over to keep Jules company while she's away. We were just sitting there eating soft pretzels, when who should come by, but BB and his guard dog, Ryan, who looks pretty much like you'd expect a paid guard to look—lots of muscle, short-short hair, and suspicious eyes. Jules sort of flirted with Ryan and I think he liked her, which is totally possible because she's so pretty and looks way older than 15. We're thinking maybe we'll invite him to the party too. That way BB can come.

While Jules distracted Ryan, BB and I drifted off to another table. It was <u>so nice</u> to see him outside school. I told him about the New Year's party, and he said he can't believe it, but his dad is forcing him to go to Philadelphia for the whole Xmas vacation, and Ryan is going too. I think it will be terrible for him because his stepmom hates him. We both were so bummed. I started crying on the spot and had to use napkins from the pretzel stand to blow my nose a hundred times.

<u>W3TP: Why do I judge Ms. Gardner on her appearance when I would hate it if anyone did that to me? Bad Sadie, bad.</u>
Posted 12/16 at 8:20 PM

2 URock 1 ITalk

awwww . . . BB's 2 cute 2 be a sociopath nd Ryan iz hot in hiz own militaristic He-Man way. Do u rilly think he likes me?
Posted 12/17 at 1 AM by nujules4u

Wednesday, December 22

Today BB and I skipped last period and exchanged Xmas presents, since he is leaving first thing tomorrow to go to his dad's. OMG, he got me something way cool. It's a silver waist chain that fits me perfectly, with a tiny silver heart. When he put it on me I thought my skin would blister where he touched me—his fingers almost burned. If we weren't in the park, who knows what might have happened? Of course, that provoked tears and more hair stroking—luckily I do have the good kind of hair that is soft and not frizzy like WS's, so it's nice to touch. I could sit for hours with my head on his shoulder and have him comfort me.

We already resolved that next semester (if we stay in school), we'll stop skipping our afternoon classes because if he's a *good boy* his dad says he'll stop paying Ryan to live with him. (BB thinks his dad just wants to save the money.)

That leaves the problem of Mr. H, who can still get to BB in a way no one else can. This AM we were standing by my locker, maybe a little too close (but nothing every other couple in school doesn't do), when Mr. H walked by and stopped and said, "No touching, Mr. B," and BB almost went berserk. I had to hold back both of his arms and remind him that he doesn't need any more trouble. He got mad at me then and ripped up all the index cards with the anger-management tips on them and threw them at me. That really hurt my feelings even if a lot of the ideas were lame, but he even pushed Ronzo out of the way right after that, so I realized just how stressful BB's life is right now.

Then I got sadder because I realized how soon we would be separated again. How will I get through 11 days without my sweetie? He did promise to try and call whenever he can. Of course, I am about the only kid in tenth grade without a cell phone, so the only number he can call is the same one I share with WS and MOM. Sigh.

W3TP: Trying to have an even semi-happy holiday without the person you love most in the world.
Posted 12/22 at 7:09 PM

o URock o ITalk

Thursday, December 23

Today, WS, MOM, Aunt Sara, and me exchanged our presents, because MOM leaves tomorrow on her cruise that Aunt Sara is paying for. (That would never happen with me and WS!) They're flying to Florida and then sailing around Mexico and other places like that for a week. MOM's really excited—almost as much as I am about Jules's party. Her excitement made me realize it must be tough to be my MOM, dealing with two daughters and a job that is supposed to be eight hours a day but always ends up being ten. Worst of all is having your husband dump you for a Mabel.

WS says if Mabel comes to our house, she will call the police and tell them she's a suspected child abuser. I didn't tell her or MOM that Mabel emailed me a couple times, just stupid stuff, like once a chain letter and another time a picture of my dad riding a motorcycle, which I showed to BB. He thought the bike was so cool and wants DAD to bring it out here and take him for a ride.

W3TP: Feeling guilty because your DAD's girlfriend wants to be your best friend, even though you haven't done anything to encourage her.
Posted 12/23 at 7:55 PM

2 URock o ITalk

Saturday, December 25

Another Xmas and no cell phone! I can't believe it—I even promised to get a job to pay for the monthly fee, but DAD said he thought I was still *too young.* WS doesn't have one either, but that's by choice—she did a school report on how cell phones cause brain cancer, so she doesn't want one. Not only is she goth, she's weird goth—or is that an oxymoron? (See, Sadie does pay attention in English.)

I did get some good stuff, though, like a gift certificate for clothes and some new CDs and books, so it wasn't too bad. Homer was the center of attention because I got him a squeaky toy that he wouldn't stop playing with—and I tied a Santa hat on him. So cute!

Jules called and told me her parents got her a diamond bracelet that is so valuable Mona is going to put it in a safety deposit box along with the solid-gold necklace they got her for her birthday. It sucks majorly that she has to be away from them, but it totally rocks to get that kind of present. She didn't say what Mona or Abby got from them.

Best of all, BB called to tell me he loves me more than ever and that his favorite Christmas present was the sound of my voice telling him I still love him and will never even think of being with another boy. (He doesn't know my stupid ex seems obsessed with me and still posts on here from time to time.)

W3TP: Christmas is never as much fun as when you're little and still believe in Santa Claus. (Thanks to WS, I stopped believing the same year she did because she was *kind* enough to share his nonexistence with me.)
Posted 12/25 at 8:30 PM

o URock o ITalk

Thursday, December 30

So bored, but tomorrow is New Year's Eve, and I get to go to Jules's and it will be all good. DAD must be missing Mabel because he calls her about four times a day, and last night I heard him ask her to fly out. (I think she said yes because he is now totally okay with me staying with Jules for New Year's.) Anyway, me and WS both listened through the bathroom door when we saw him head in there with his cell phone. WS can be funny at moments like that. She was (silently) pretending to be Mabel, rolling her eyes and sighing; it was weird too because WS never met her, but that's exactly how Mabel acts.

After DAD got off the phone, WS *accidentally*:
• Knocked over his fresh cup of coffee
• Let Homer get paw prints all over the paperwork DAD brought along to finish during vacation
• Lost his car keys in the garbage can

She also did her hilarious barfing pose whenever his back was turned. If you have a sibling, you might try it whenever you think your parents have gone too far. Your parents will get very confused because they won't know why the two of you are consumed with laughter.

WS is now speaking to DAD, thankfully, since it's been like a horror movie in our house, the kind where you keep watching and waiting for something terrible to happen between the evil monster (her) and the innocent hero (him). But DAD has been so sweet, not only getting my cereal every morning (Frooty Loops, thank you), but doing the laundry and cleaning up the house. When he made WS's favorite spaghetti like he used to, she got tears in her eyes and the tension melted just like that.

WS and Slap are spending New Year's Eve with his grandma. If that isn't weird I don't know what is, but apparently Slap's grandma likes to play cards for money and last time they did, WS won ten dollars. (Yes, a highly principled goth will rip off an old lady for money, justifying it as her college fund.) I imagine she'll want my blouse again, although sometimes she's gone *soft goth* when they visit (i.e. all black but no accessories).

The only problem is that BB hasn't been able to call, and this leaves our Jules-fest guest list with a big blank spot. But Emma is coming, so maybe it'll be a girls' night.

W3TP: A dad who spends more time thinking about his girlfriend than his daughters.
Posted 12/30 at 6:54 PM

o URock o ITalk

Saturday, January 1
Last night totally rocked. We had so much fun, even though Dustin was there. Luckily, Emma warned me beforehand that she told him he could come for *old time's sake*. (BB would

die if he knew.) I forgot how funny Dustin can be. (Although now that he is on this big Christian kick, he gets a little annoying because religion is his answer to everything except his ability to skateboard, which he still insists comes from <u>my</u> influence.) He's definitely been reading my blog because he asked to see my waist chain. (I showed everyone after having a little too much to drink.)

Jules just emailed me this pic of Dustin. She copied it from a pic Emma gave me last summer before I moved—when she thought we might get back together.

The bad part about having a ton of fun due to vodka and orange juice (I thought one might cancel out the other) is that you pay for it double the next day. When I woke up, I thought I would puke, and my head hurt worse than any headache before. But since the apartment got a little trashed, Jules and I had to clean up real quick before Mona got home.

After that, we watched *Annie*, because Abby got the DVD for Christmas. When I was little, I loved that show and my parents once took me to see the play for my birthday. Now one of the songs is on my mind, because guess who will be in my arms at this time "Tomorrow"?

<u>W3TP: Alcohol—who got that whole thing</u>

started? You feel so good you want more, but that's exactly when you should stop.
Posted 1/1 at 7:23 PM

---

6 URock 4 ITalk

hey u cute thing, u r still as luvable as ever. get ridda that bad boy nd take me back! even tho the Jesus talk is tru, i'll can it 4 u.
Posted 1/1 at 8 PM by sk8r4life

mona found a beer in the fridge nd freaked big time when she got home. i told her u stole it from ur dad, just one, nd we decided not to drink it, so stick with that story if she calls, ok?
Posted 1/1 at 8:14 PM by nujules4u

what a night! everything went rite. u sure have changed, Sades, i nevah thought u would strut ur stuff like that. it was 2 fun, when can we do it again? ur nu school wud rock if everyone was like Jules.
Posted 1/1 at 9:02 PM by ems89

Dustin, just becuz I said you were <u>sort of</u> funny doesn't mean you can start posting here all the time. I am <u>not</u> your good luck charm!
Posted 1/1 at 10:30 PM by nugrl90

Chapter Fifteen

Tuesday, January 4

Okay, I'm scared and I'm worried and I'm not sure what to do. All day I've been thinking about something that happened with BB yesterday, and twice I had to go to Poisonous Penders's because I thought my head was going to explode. (If you remember how nasty she is and how I swore I would never go to her office again, you'll realize this was a major event.)

I've even blocked a ton of people from my blog because I don't want to deal with the things some people would say, plus what I'm about to write is uber confidential. BB and I promised each other not to skip school anymore, but that was impossible this week because we hadn't seen each other in <u>forever</u>, so yesterday we decided to go to his house. (Luckily, Ryan is gone!)

After we ate all the snacks in the kitchen, which wasn't much, he said, "Come on upstairs. I have something really cool to show you."

We went up to his bedroom, which was a real mess—his mom definitely doesn't care about stuff like cleaning. He made me sit on the bed and close my eyes while he got this little suitcase out from underneath.

"Okay, you can look," he said, and then I saw that inside the box was a gun and a bunch of stuff that goes with it. That's right—a REAL GUN.

"Where did you get that?" I gasped. I've never seen a gun that close before.

"I took it from my dad's house. He has so many he'll never notice. I hid it in the car on the way home. So, what do you think? Want to hold it?"

"Brian, why do you need a gun?" I asked. Until then I was hoping, just hoping, it might be fake, but when he took all the parts out of the box and snapped them together, it was pretty obvious it wasn't—and that he knew how to use it.

"Come on, just hold it," he said. "My dad took me to the shooting range on vacation, and this baby feels really good in your hands."

"Why in the world do you want a gun?" I asked him again. "You'll get into so much trouble if anyone finds out!"

"Not if you don't tell. This is between you and me," he said. "Anyway, I figure you'll never break up with me now."

He laughed, but not in a happy way.

"That's not funny," I told him, but he got all serious and asked if I was thinking of breaking up with him. Then, just as quick, he said, "psyche, gotcha," like he was kidding.

When he realized he wasn't going to get me to touch the gun, he took it apart and put it back in the box. He seemed disappointed that I wasn't all enthusiastic about it and said it was a special gun called a Glock, which I later looked up online and found out is really dangerous.

I got upset—a little at first, but then more as time went on. I asked BB again why he needed a gun and started crying. I said, "You can mess up your life big time if you get caught, not to mention our relationship." I thought he would hug me and pat my hair like usual, but instead he grabbed my shoulders and shook me really hard.

He said, "Don't be so stupid, Sadie. Don't you realize how many assholes there are in the world?"

It really hurt both my bones and my feelings, so I ran out of the house crying. He came after me and said he was sorry, and we made up pretty fast because I can't stay upset with someone who loves me so much.

I told him to never bring that gun to school. He said it didn't really work anymore, but I knew that was a lie to try and calm me down. He had looked too proud of it when he first showed it to me. I said, "If it really is broken, we should bury it somewhere or dump it in a trash can." He turned on some music like I was totally boring and told me to chill out.

CHILL OUT!!!!!! My BBF steals a gun and thinks I should chill out? I think I could be named an accessory or something if he shot someone. OMG, I can't even believe I wrote that.

After that I pretty much just wanted to go home, but it was only 2:00, so I had to wait for WS to get out of school at 2:45. For the first time in my life, I was actually glad to see her.

On the drive home, I asked her if Slap was ever violent, and she got this detective look on her face and asked me what was going on, but I said nothing. She screeched the car over to the side and asked if this was about Brian. I said no, it was about nothing, let's just go home. She waited in silence for a couple of minutes because she knows she can usually break me with this tactic, but I stared out the car window and refused to talk.

W3TP: Guns: how do they protect you when you end up in jail for using them? Or worse?
Posted 1/4 at 4:30 PM

---

o URock 3 ITalk

Sadie, u r way craze 2 deal with a gun, either make him get rid of it or dump him—pronto! 2 many of my friends got shot in NYC—itz terrible 2 c that.
Posted 1/4 at 4:35 PM by nujules4u

u need 2 do sumthin soon, grl. i agree with Jules, this is nutz. if u don't tell sumone, I will. I don't want to c u hurt.
Posted 1/4 at 4:45 PM by sk8r4life

Sades, i have 2 agree. this could b real trouble—talk 2 ur mom

right now! Wut if he shoots up the school?
Posted 1/4 at 4:50 PM by ems89

Wednesday, January 5

Can't sleep. Neither can Homer. Here is what his paw types:
mmmmmmmmmmmmmmmmxmxmmmmmmmmmxmxmxm
xmxmxmxm

I keep trying to breathe deeply and go into a tranquil state of sleep, like Ms. Armstrong suggested once, but I can't. The memory of that gun is like having a song stuck in my mind. On the phone tonight I told BB I thought I <u>would</u> have to break up with him because it was making me too crazy with worry. Those are words I never thought I'd say.

BB got real silent and then, even worse, he started to cry—and guy cry is the worst kind of cry there is, if you've ever heard it. Right now, he is so bummed because his dad said BB can't visit anymore because his stepmom hates him so much. My poor BB is struggling with so many things at once, and no one but me will listen—how can I abandon him?

I know I need to tell an adult about the gun, but if I do, it might mean the end of my relationship with BB. I already know BB won't understand. I've been surfing for information all night and here's what I found:
<u>http://www.safeyouth.org/scripts/teens/firearm.asp</u>

They pretty much say you <u>have</u> to tell, but I don't even know Ms. Miller, my guidance counselor, that well because I saw her only once when I was sent down to her office for missing too many afternoon classes. She is okay, I guess, but what if she doesn't believe me? I could send an anonymous tip, but BB will know who did it, I'm sure. Ryan has crawled back into whatever hole he came out of, so he won't be any help.

W3TP: A sweet guy who steals a gun. (He finally admitted it's real but said he won't ever use it.)
Posted 1/6 at 1:30 AM

o URock 1 ITalk

where were u 2day? are u ok? i had 2 eat lunch all by myself nd it sucked. every time i saw BB i just wanted to hide. i even thought he might have hurt u, but then i saw ur sis nd she said u stayed home becuz of a headache. IM me!
Posted 1/6 at 4:07 PM by nujules4u

Thursday, January 6
I was too tired to go to school today after being up all night. MOM got majorly pissed when I refused to get out of bed, but at least I got some sleep finally. Homer and I got up just in time for all the soaps, so I ate popcorn and pretended I was one of the people on the TV, to see if I could figure out what to do.

When BB called me today from school, I tried to act like nothing was wrong but I was totally nervous about talking to him. We didn't have much to say, but he promised me he will never do anything with the you-know-what.

This whole gun thing has made me think a lot about the shivery excited feelings I've had about BB—like when he convinced me to skip school to show I would get in trouble for him, or when he shoved that guy against the lockers for asking to borrow my English notes, or how he sometimes jerks on my waist chain so hard it hurts. All these things seemed like love at the time, but now I wonder—especially because MOM has a lot of domestic violence clients she can't stop talking about. They all think the person who beat them up or broke their bones loved them too.

And then there's the way BB looks at Mr. Hammacker every morning. It's been getting worse and worse lately. If Mr. H humiliates him in class or tells us, *No PDA!* one more time, I'm afraid BB will use that gun to shoot Mr. H—maybe not to death, but just to teach him a lesson. BB seems to brag to me about not *taking crap from people* more and more.

My conclusion: BB is not the type of person to shoot other kids or me, but if he did hurt Mr. H and I could have stopped it, I'd feel guilty probably for the rest of my life. But what a choice: to rat on BB and lose my BBF over a person I don't even like.

W3TP: You love someone, he scares you, you love someone, he scares you. . . .
Posted 1/6 at 3:05 PM

o URock 3 ITalk

Superchick—think real quick—member when u slept over on Xmas break nd i saw the mark on ur waist nd u said BB was just kidding around? i didn't want 2 say anything then, but i will now: that didn't look like kidding! And what about that other time when I saw those bruises on ur arm where he grabbed u?
Posted 1/6 at 6 PM by ems89

Ems, you don't understand—those times he really <u>was</u> fooling around. Don't post about that stuff anymore—Slap is getting on my case and threatening to tell ykw.
Posted 1/6 at 6:10 PM by nugrl90

Sadie, please come to skool 2morrow!
Posted 1/6 at 6:12 PM by nujules4u

Chapter Sixteen

Saturday, January 8

So this is what happened. Thursday night on the phone, BB told me that at school Mr. Hammacker whispered under his breath: "I'm going to take you down, mister." All BB's friends were there, and even though they didn't hear it, they saw how disrespectful Mr. H was to him. BB was plenty steamed about what happened, but I promised to come back to school and give him a big hug.

Which is what I did. On Friday morning, he came running up to meet me as soon as WS pulled in the parking lot, and once she was out of sight, I grabbed him and squeezed as hard as I could.

"I love you soooo much," I said, but then when I went to put my arm around him, I noticed something felt funny in his backpack, and asked him: "Brian, what is that?"

He put one finger across his lips and said, "Shhh," and then unzipped his backpack and there was the box with the gun.

I immediately got all shaky, like when you have a really bad fever and can't get warm enough. "Brian, please tell me that box is empty," I said. I could hear the quiver in my voice.

"Don't worry, I won't use it," he said, and mussed up my hair a little like he does when he's fooling around. "I just brought it to show Ronzo." Then he kind of jogged away, waving good-bye as he headed to homeroom.

Since I was absent on Wednesday and Thursday, I had to go to the principal's office with a stupid permission slip—to be allowed back in school. (Would they really refuse to let me in if I didn't have one?) While I was waiting in line in the office, thinking about that gun, my head started pounding so bad I couldn't stand it. I kind of slumped down in a chair that's supposed to be reserved for important people like parents and visitors, and closed my eyes.

Ms. Turner, our principal, happened to be walking in the office just then. When she saw me in the chair, she came over, and I thought she was about to yell at me, but I must have looked pretty bad because instead she asked if everything was okay.

That was the wrong question to ask. Her voice was so soft and nice that I started to cry, and she quickly brought me in her office. I knew I had to tell her about the gun, but my heart was breaking because ratting BB out is something he would never forgive.

Getting started was like the first time I went off a high dive; I just talked myself into taking one step forward, knowing every-thing else would happen automatically. And it did. I guess some part of me was thinking I could actually help BB and save our relationship, because he really is a good person living under bad circumstances, with an anger management problem that can be helped.

Once I got to the part about the gun, Ms. Turner was like a movie on fast forward. She called the police while she was figuring out on her computer which class BB was in. (I could have told her it was Geometry if I wasn't sobbing so hard.) The next thing you know, the cops were there and BB was pulled out of class. (I heard later that everybody was screaming and hiding under their desks when the cops burst into the room.)

Luckily, I didn't have to see him because Ms. Turner let me stay in her office. Everyone said he was fighting and cursing as the police dragged him out in handcuffs.

No one knows what happened after that, but the newspaper today said he would be going to juvenile detention at the very least, and maybe even worse. The article also mentioned that *another student* turned BB in. If he sees it, I'm sure he'll know it was me.

After BB got taken out, Ms. Turner told me I did the right thing and called my guidance counselor to come and talk to me. Ms. Miller ended up being better than I thought. She made some tea for me in her office, and even though I didn't really like the taste, it was nice to have someone at school treat me like I was special.

Then, the school called MOM and there was a lot of drama. She came running into Ms. Miller's office and swept me up into her arms.

"Oh Sadie, my poor precious baby," she sobbed. Her eyes were so puffed up I could tell she had been crying ever since she heard the news. "I was so worried! I heard there was a shooter at the school, and I didn't even know you were involved when I jumped in my car and headed over. Then my cell phone rang, and I found out it was that awful Brian who had the gun."

"Mom, please—" I tried to explain, but she had me smashed against her chest so tight I could barely breathe, let alone talk.

"Sadie, I promise, we're going to work this out," she went on. I didn't like the sound of that. Hadn't I just done that very thing?

Before I could object, she got me out of the school and into her car. We went home, and after she wore herself out lecturing me, she said I was brave to do what I did. I asked if she would have done it too, even if it meant losing her BBF ever, and she just hugged me and said she hoped she would have. Sometimes my MOM seems so busy with her life and unaware of mine, but other times I can tell she really does remember how awful it is to be a teenager and in love and deprived of your boyfriend.

I expected WS to lay into me about what happened, but miracle of miracles, she offered to drive me to see Emma in person so I could talk about *things.* But actually, I was too scared to leave the house because I didn't know then that BB was locked up. I never thought he would hurt me, but then I never thought he'd steal a gun or bring it to school, and I imagine he's madder at me now than he ever was at Mr. Hammacker.

DAD almost had a coronary when he found out, especially because he met Brian and thought he was an okay kid. He said obviously I wasn't completely truthful about my relationship with him or DAD would have known he wasn't. After a twenty-minute "How could you upset your family like this?" phone call, he sent me three emails and called back twice, asking if I'm okay. He's also planning on coming home this week.

Then, as if I hadn't been reamed out enough already, Aunt Sara showed up, looking all stern and serious and sad. She didn't say a word. She didn't even take off her coat. She just came right over to me and hugged me really hard for a long time.

Finally, after all the awfulness ended, the strangest thing happened: BB's dad called to thank me for what I did. He told me that he's been worried about BB for a long time, especially since last summer, when BB had some *run-ins* with the law. He thought things were getting better, which is why he stopped having Ryan around all the time, but now he realizes they weren't. He said he blames himself for not locking up the guns better.

W3TP: Having a story that should happen only in movies be your real life.
Posted 1/8 at 7:18 PM

6 URock o ITalk

Thursday, January 20
I've finally found the energy to post again. Now that I'm back, I've unblocked everyone, since all my secrets are out anyway.

I still love BB with every part of my being and miss him like crazy. Everyone at school (including some of Mia's friends, if you can believe that) has been treating me like some kind of hero(ine) and thanking me for turning him in. In a way I wish I had never done it—but it turns out the gun was loaded, which REALLY makes me wonder if I knew him at all.

And now you wouldn't even know that BB ever went to our school because all signs of him are gone. His locker is cleaned out, and after the reporters stopped coming around, it's like any other normal week at school. Except it's not.

Meanwhile, I'm still wearing my waist chain and his gold necklace.

W3TP: Having someone so totally a part of your life vanish completely.
Posted 1/20 at 5:20 PM

---

20 URock 6 ITalk

i kno u feel bad about wut happened, but u had no choice. u need 2 come 2 my church becuz u cud be helped by the pastor there. he is way cool nd not like what u might think. promise me u'll think about it, even if u don't want 2 see me.
Posted 1/20 at 5:25 PM by sk8r4life

Sades—u ARE so brave—think of all the lives u saved! ur like a movie star becuz of all that's happened. i can't believe it, u must be in shock. i told my mom nd she wuz so proud of u. in fact, she sez if u want, u can come stay with us this summer nd get away from everything there. call me nd we can talk about it, ok?
Posted 1/20 at 5:30 PM by ems89

No matter what has happened, I want to say that I think you are an amazing person. I think I probably loved BB like you until my parents made me break up with him. He hurt me but I still wanted to be with him, he has that effect on you. When my old buds emailed me about everything that happened, I thought wow, that would be so tough because my parents were in charge of what happened to me, but you didn't have anyone. Someday he will know you really truly cared for him.
Posted 1/20 at 5:40 PM by uduntknome

Sades, hang in there, u'll c life will get back 2 normal, wutever that is. don't worry, i told everyone the rumors Mia is spreading about u being pregnant r so not tru.
Posted 1/20 at 5:45 PM by nujules4u

Okay, you're asking for it, Jules. For the record, I did NOT start any rumors about Sadie! I wasn't going to let anyone in on your little *secret* cause I didn't want to cause more problems for Sadie, but this is too much to let pass. My mom happened to meet your sister at the pediatrician's office last week when she took my little brother in for a checkup, and GUESS WHAT WORLD—Jules, you are a big liar and fake. Your mom is really a crack addict and your dad doesn't even exist. That crock of lies you told me and Sadie was just to try and impress us. I bet you don't even have a boyfriend at all. What is wrong with you?
Posted 1/20 at 6:05 PM by kool2Bmia

Sades—IM me!
Posted 1/20 at 6:10 PM by nujules4u

Monday, January 24

I can barely drag myself off the sofa to write this, let alone go to school. Tomorrow night MOM is forcing me to go see Dr. White, who works with her—apparently she thinks I am *seriously depressed.*

Seriously depressed—why would I be? First, the boy I think I want to spend the rest of my life with turns out to be some kind of psychopath (that's what the newspaper said, anyway), and I didn't even know it until he went extreme on me.

Then, my new VBF turns out to be a total fraud—yes, what Mia wrote is true. After I read it, I made WS drive me over to Jules's right away, but Jules was at work, so I asked Mona.

In reality, there is:
- No diamond bracelet or solid-gold necklace
- No opera singer dad
- No hand model mom
- No private school in Manhattan
- No boyfriend about to become a famous rapper

I never really talked to Mona alone before, but WS actually played with Abby so we could have some privacy. Mona tried to explain that Jules has had a really unhappy childhood and was even in foster care for a while before she came to stay with Mona. Still, I felt so hurt and told Mona to have Jules call me as soon as she got home. She did, and we had a huge fight:

"Jules, how could you lie to me like that?" I said (well, really, yelled) into the phone. "How shallow do you think I am to need friends who are rich or famous?"

"You say that, Sadie, but all you talked about the first week of school was how broke your family was. It was so obvious that you're all about status!" she shouted back, like her lies were all my fault.

It went on from there, back and forth with neither of us being willing to admit we had done something wrong. Finally, she started crying, and then I started crying, and we both had to hang up.

At least Homer will always be there for me—I think.

W3TP: Friends who think they need to have a life like a movie in order for you to like them.
Posted 1/24 at 7:24 PM

---

20 URock 3 ITalk

It wuzn't about u nd i didn't want to hurt u. when we met u were having hard times with ur mom nd dad splitting up, so i thot u wudn't want 2 hear about all the things that have gone wrong in my life. nd just like u i wuz worried about being a nu grl in a school where every1 already had friends.
Posted 1/24 at 7:30 PM by nujules4u

It sounds to me like you <u>both</u> need to forgive and forget. I did that with BB and all the ignorant people at school who started rumors that I was pregnant too. (Why is that the first thing people say when a girl has problem?) w/e.
Posted 1/24 at 7:42 PM by uduntknome

Superslick, superchick: i think Jules is a nice person even if she did make a mistake, we all do. remember when u told me in 4th grade that ur dad was an undercover agent 4 the CIA? nd sometimes i wasn't completely honest with u either, like when i told u that CF kissed me at the football game behind the bleachers. well he didn't (even tho i really wished 4 it!) call me if u need to talk!!!!

Posted 1/24 at 7:45 PM by ems89

Chapter Seventeen

Tuesday, February 1

Tonight was my second visit with Dr. White, the lame therapist
my MOM works with. After an hour with him, I am rethinking
my desire to be a psychologist because, clearly, he knows
nothing about kids or what it's like to have your life shattered by
someone you love. Yes, I guess you could say I am now angry
with BB, angry because he ruined the beautiful thing we had
together and angry because he scared me so bad with the stupid
gun and angry because he turned out to be what everyone said
he was.

BB is gone, but I have to see Jules every day. Part of the huge
crack in my heart is because of her. I thought she was so funny
and truthful and talented and loyal. Now I just think about all the
stories (lies) she told me. I've been going to the library during
lunch and haven't talked to her since our big confrontation, but
WS says I should give her another chance (we actually had a
talk about it, if you can believe that) and Emma does too.

W3TP: Relationships that seem so real and turn out to be so false and wrong.
Posted 2/1 at 11:57 PM

10 URock o ITalk

Friday, February 4

Tonight DAD called and talked nonstop. (Although, note that he cancelled his trip home to lecture me in person because Mabel had some kind of breakdown, but no details on that yet). Apparently he and MOM are seriously considering sending me to a private school, where I'll be more closely supervised.

"Sadie, it would be a good thing all around," he told me. "It might even improve your grades—I know you are better than a D student."

What makes him think I even care about school, let alone my grades?

It was one of those DAD autopilot conversations where I don't have to say a word and he keeps on talking, even if I put the phone down on the counter and just look at it. After I finally escaped, MOM got on the phone and they talked real low so I couldn't hear what they were saying. WS told me she thinks MOM has a new boyfriend from the cruise, which is just too gross to think about. Two parents dating—tgfw.

W3TP: Getting so much attention when you mess up, but not when you do things right.
Posted 2/4 at 7:10 PM

4 URock o ITalk

Tuesday, February 8

When Dr. White talks about me, it's like he's talking about another person.

Here are some of his *observations*:
- I am guilty of truancy.
- My school performance is abysmal.
- I deceive my parents.
- I engage in high-risk behaviors.

This makes me sound so bad, like a criminal or worse. I want to ask him why he doesn't just send me off to jail and be done with it. (Maybe I would see BB there, since someone at school said that's where he is. What would I say if I did??)

I told MOM seeing a doctor is a complete waste of money, but she says DAD and her agreed that I need professional help. According to Dr. White, I have been depressed for a long time, as evidenced by my *somatic* headaches and general lack of happiness. I didn't tell him that I've had headaches all my life, but they got really bad about the time MOM and DAD started screaming at each other nonstop. Anyway, who wouldn't prefer lying on the sofa with Homer and watching TV over seeing a shrink and going to school where everyone stares at you?

W3TP: Parents who think they can give their kids all kinds of advice when their own lives are a mess!
Posted 2/8 at 9:03 PM

3 URock 0 ITalk

Monday, February 14

Today they were selling carnations for Valentine's Day at school, and Jules came up to me all smiley faced and gave me one with a really sweet card about how much she cares for me. That melted the part of my heart that was still hard against her, but it will be a long time before I believe anything she says. And then there is the hurt that will never go away: BB. He would have bought me a dozen carnations.

W3TP: Not having a sweetheart on Valentine's Day. 😞 😞 😞
Posted 2/14 at 4:05 PM

8 URock 1 ITalk

ahem. remember who bot u 3 red roses last year? seriously, im praying 4 u.
Posted 2/14 at 4:15 PM by sk8r4life

Tuesday, February 15

It's been almost a month since I found out the truth about Jules. I guess she and I are finally going to try to be friends again. After my last post, I started thinking about how much her life must suck—just like mine, or maybe even worse. So last night I got her some candy and fixed it up in a pair of really cute socks with hearts on them and gave it to her in school today.

W3TP: Making a career out of sleeping—is it normal to take a nap every day when you're a teenager?

Posted 2/15 at 3:34 PM

4 URock 1 ITalk

hey grl, i think we shud get 2gether this weekend nd talk. IM me, we can meet at the mall.
Posted 2/15 at 4 PM by nujules4u

Wednesday, February 16

I didn't feel like doing anything even remotely fun tonight, but WS forced me to go to the mall by being so mean I begged MOM to let me out of the house.

Emma and Dustin just happened to be there (is it possible that WS clued them in because she felt sorry for me?), so we hung out, and for the first time since that gun came into my life, I felt a little bit happy. Dustin made me laugh so hard I spit out a whole mouthful of soda all over myself. Emma made up a poem about me in under two minutes:

I have a friend named superchick
To meet her is to like her real quick
She loves to write and tell her tale
Someday her books will be on sale
The girl I'm describing is my VBF Sadie
Not just a friend, but an incredible lady
Her kindness and talent will take her very far
She can't see it now, but someday she'll be a star.

W3TP: Sisters who try to persecute you and end up helping you.
Posted 2/16 at 10:45 PM

Monday, February 21

I discovered that going to Ms. Miller's office is way better than going to the school nurse because she acts like she's actually happy to see me, not as much as Ms. Armstrong, but still better than Poisonous Penders. I can go to the guidance office as much as I want, and if Ms. Miller doesn't have time to see me, she still lets me sit and do my homework or read a magazine so I can have a break from classes.

Today in her office she suggested I make a list of things upsetting me, so here is My Unhappiness List:

1. You can guess what number one is.
2. Being deceived by a girl you thought was the strongest and bravest person you knew. (The last part might still be true—she really did have an awful life and doesn't even know where her mom is now.)
3. My MOM *does* have a boyfriend she met on the Christmas cruise. His name is Charlie—eww—and she talks to him on the phone almost every night. WS says they meet each other for lunch at work almost every day too. He has <u>white</u> hair!
4. A DAD who cancels a trip to see his *disturbed* daughter at the last minute in order to stay at the bedside of his *disturbed* girlfriend. (It turns out Mabel has an ulcer, not mental problems.)
5. My sister isn't so bad these days, but now, when I thought she'd finally leave for college, she thinks *maybe* she will live at home and commute.
6. I have only one old VBF and one sort of VBF, but no other BFs or just friends.

7. Dr. White and MOM and DAD and Aunt Sara and almost everyone else think I should go on antidepressants. I don't want to because that will mean I'm crazy. The next thing you know, I'll be in that special school MOM was looking up on the web. (Of course, everyone knows those kids aren't *special,* they're rejects who don't fit in anywhere else.)

8. My grades suck, and now Ms. Gardner won't let me write for the school paper until I'm passing everything.

9. Aunt Sara has been out of town for a long time, working on a special assignment. Even though she sent me a bunch of funny postcards and calls me, I still miss her.

10. I don't really have a tenth thing, but a list of nine is wrong.

When I was done, Ms. Miller suggested I tear it up to *release* my sadness, so I did. Why, then, did I retype it all out here?

W3TP: Having more unhappiness than happiness in your life— the Happiness List might have 3 things: Homer and Aunt Sara and my VBFs.
Posted 2/21 at 3:45 PM

2 URock o ITalk

Monday, February 28

Aunt Sara just got back from her assignment and has all these exciting stories about Europe that really make me think the whole psychologist thing isn't right for me. She told me if I become a writer, I can live a life that is way cool like hers. Plus, she brought me a stack of teen magazines from every country she visited so I can see what girls around the world are like. (Of course, she picked the *junior* versions with some teenybopper kind of stuff, and it made me realize how everyone in my family sees me as a little girl, when I'm not.)

After my appointment with Dr. White tonight, Aunt Sara and I went to the mall for pizza and I saw Dustin there. She let us hang out together while she did some shopping. We went to the arcade and played video games (featuring skaters) until all our money was gone. Sometimes he is really fun, especially when he doesn't go o&o about me being his good luck charm or bug me to come to his church and meet his pastor (who happens to be a skate-boarder too—how weird is that?)

W3TP: European girls seem totally cool, not unhappy or obsessed with their bodies or boyfriends like American girls.
Posted 2/28 at 9:34 PM

4 URock 1 ITalk

i think abut it 2. u r as hot as evah, maybe more.
Posted 2/28 at 10 PM by sk8r4life

Friday, March 4
I'm literally shaking as I type this.

When I got home from school today, there in the mailbox was a letter from BB. I could tell right away it was his handwriting, so I grabbed it and locked myself in the bathroom to read it in peace. Luckily, Homer had chewed off the top of one of WS's combat boots, so she was too busy yelling at him to notice me. (Side note: Yelling at Homer only gets him excited and makes him bark with happiness, but WS hasn't figured that out yet.)

Anyway, my hands could barely open the envelope. I thought it would be either really nice, which would make me love him all over again, or really evil, which would make me afraid he would come and shoot me when he got out, but it was neither. In fact, I bet somebody forced him to write that letter and had read it over before letting him send it. Here is what he wrote:

Sadie:

Just wanted to let you know that I am doing well here and will soon finish my GED. Since I'm suspended from high school forever, I am going to take college courses until I'm 18 and then go in the military so my record will be wiped.

I am in a twelve-step program here because I admitted I have anger management problems and abuse alcohol and am powerless to help myself. I've learned that I have expressed my feelings by violence instead of in more healthy ways. One of the things I have to do is make amends to those I've wronged, so I'm writing to Ms. Turner, Mr. H, and you.

I am sorry for all the problems I caused you. I know you are emotionally disturbed yourself, and my problems made it worse for you. It was a mistake for us to ever hook up, I know now, but that is in the past and we have to let go of it and move on.

So you and I will probably never see each other again, because after I get out of here I'm going to live with my uncle in California and start over. My mom is just as relieved to be rid of me, but I don't really care about that.

Sincerely,

Brian

P.S. Could you please return my gold-chain necklace and all the video games I let you borrow?

I bet they forced BB to take some kind of medicine, which is exactly why I won't take Dr. W's drugs—they make you brain-washed and weird and not yourself. BB clearly isn't himself. What we had was real, not some big mistake. The worst thing in the world you can do is tell someone your relationship was wrong when the last time you spoke to her, you said, *I love you so much I ache.* I don't know whether to write back a really nasty letter, ignore him, or cry my eyes out. WS drove me to his house so I could leave his stuff (including the waist chain) in the mail-box—as if I would want it now!

W3TP: Someone who brought a gun to school suggesting someone else is *emotionally disturbed!* Go figure.
Posted 3/4 at 10:57 PM

Chapter Eighteen

Sunday, March 6

I am <u>so</u> depressed. The future looks all bad to me. Every morning I can barely drag myself out of bed, and I wonder if it's even worth it to go on. Not that I would kill myself, even though Dr. White keeps asking me. MOM told him she thinks I'm getting more depressed. Aunt Sara seems worried too—she took me to the movies to try and cheer me up (along with a secret agenda of trying to convince me to take medicine to make me un-depressed). This was the final blow because Aunt Sara can usually be counted on to side with me on everything in a cool sort of way.

<u>Reasons Not to Take Happy Pills</u>
They're expensive—even with insurance (this I know from MOM's job)
I heard they make you sleepy
They are chemicals and unnatural
I don't want my mind controlled
They can't fix a broken heart

<u>Reasons to Take Happy Pills</u>
People will stop nagging me
Maybe I won't get headaches anymore
Lots of kids take them
Maybe they can make a heart a little less broken

W3TP: Being betrayed by one of the few adults you think you can really relate to, especially when you are duped into thinking she just wants to spend a *fun* evening with you.
Posted 3/6 at 10:01 PM

10 URock 3 ITalk

O Sadie, i just want 2 give u a big hug nd let u kno how much i care about u. IM me rite now!
Posted 3/6 at 10:15 PM by nujules4u

hey, Sades, no matter wut that dude said, u r awesum nd altho we broke up i still think that. IM me 2—like rite now! I kno u r a wonderful person who wants to help others like u did me.
Posted 3/6 at 10:25 PM by sk8r4life

i agree with all that's been said, don't let it do a number on ur head. u r the best no matter what any1 sez. IM me!
Posted 3/6 at 10:42 PM by ems89

Thursday, March 10

Emotionally disturbed! 😖 😖 I am so angry about BB and his stupid letter. Who does he think he is, passing judgment on me like that? Every boy I know is so superior to BB at this point— Slap looks like Prince Charming, and Dustin too.

If (and just IF) I was going to write back to BB, here is what I would say:

Dear Lyin' Brian:
It's hard to believe the military would take you, although you are

interested in guns. I think you are totally deceiving yourself about the past: you are clearly angry with your dad, who looks a lot like Mr. Hammacker, and that's why you got so hot to hurt him. I didn't want to believe you beat up or hurt other people before we met, but now I do; in fact, I think you are an excellent actor, because for a while I thought you loved me, and I deluded myself into loving you back. Calling me emotionally disturbed is so hypocritical. I'm not the one in a reform school, though, am I?
So not yours,
Sadie.

Of course I will never send this letter, which is only one of ten versions I wrote in school today. That would be a good book: <u>One Hundred Letters to Scumbag Ex-Boyfriends</u>.

Today after school, Slap and I were walking Homer while WS fed her face. (Slap likes Homer a lot and even takes him for a walk by himself sometimes.) We were just randomly talking when he said all of a sudden that there are lots of worse things that could happen to me than antidepressants. He told me the names of a few kids at my old school who were on them, and they're <u>so</u> not people you'd suspect. I'm sworn to secrecy about who it is, but according to Slap, it really helped these kids to feel better.

Somehow, we got into this big philosophical discussion about fitting in (or not) and dealing with difficulty, and I started to see the wisdom of his words. When we got back home he (horror of horrors) asked WS if she thought I should go on antidepressants. I almost ran screaming from the room until I remembered that she is anti-computer and anti-cell phone for health reasons (even though she smokes—g/f), which made me curious about her answer. I realized she's the only one in the family who never gave her opinion on the subject.

She was eating grapes and reading the newspaper and didn't even bother to look up, but she said: "Yeah—like yesterday." Then she wadded up the paper and threw it at Slap.

They started laughing and semi-wrestling and tickling each other, which usually drives me insane (think: *Goths gone wild*) but this time it actually made me jealous. Whatever else I think about Slap and WS, they are happy together, and miracle of miracles, WS was really nice to me the rest of the evening.

W3TP: Hating people you liked and liking people you hated.
Posted 3/10 at 3:23 PM

---

2 URock 1 ITalk

i'll b ur prinz any day. hey there is a lockdown at my church this weekend, if u want 2 come nd Jules 2, she wud be perfect 4 my BF Jason
Posted 3/10 at 4 PM by sk8r4life

Friday, March 11
Last night, Aunt Sara came over, and after a few glasses of wine, she told me how she was not only a bad student in high school, but the *goth* of her day (only they called them beatniks then.) If anyone could have had as many problems as me in tenth grade, it might be her.

"Sadie, if they had antidepressants for kids back then like they do now, your grandparents would have tied me down and forced me to take a truckload of them," she said, which was kind of a funny image. "But trying the pills wouldn't mean you have to take them for life—just until things start to settle down. You have to admit it's been tough lately."

So I did it. I decided to take the medicine Dr. White has been pushing. Dustin told me one of his good friends takes an anti-depressant, and after talking to him and Slap, I think maybe it could help me. Anyway, the pills are blue and white, and since blue is my favorite color (and also my state of mind), I'll give it a try.

W3TP: Everyone seems to be on antidepressants—so why is it such a big deal for me to take them?
Posted 3/11 at 7:55 PM

10 URock 1 ITalk

taking a pill when ur ill is no problem, supersister. Remember when my mom got real depressed after my brother was born nd had 2 take medicine? It really helped her. (xcept she was rite 2 be upset about my bro—he is a pitb)
Posted 3/11 at 8:05 PM by ems89

Chapter Nineteen

Tuesday, March 15

Me and Jules went to the lockdown (not like it sounds, though you do stay overnight) at Dustin's church Saturday night and it was over the top. We had so much fun—it wasn't about religion, we just hung out all night long. Jules did get along with Jason, who is actually a new guy at my old school, if you can believe that. At about four in the morning Dustin and I started talking about all the good times we had together, but it was funny because we were both so tired it was like we were drunk or something (as if that would ever happen at church!). (Mental note: Ask DAD what he was thinking when he drove my BBF out of my life.)

The pastor spent about an hour talking to me about BB because I guess Dustin clued him in on that, but we didn't get into any of the God stuff and it wasn't like my appointments with Dr. White, who keeps his pen in his hands at ALL times, ready to write down anything meaningful that I might say. Finally Pastor Ken said, "Wow, the next time I'm ready to try a new scary move on my skateboard, you'll be my inspiration, Sadie." That's when I got uncomfortable and said I needed to go call my MOM, which was a semi-lie. (She did tell me to call if I had any problems.) Is it a double sin to be dishonest to a pastor?

Today, me, Dustin, Emma, and Jules decided that we'd all apply for jobs as counselors at Camp Winetaka. Everyone except Jules should get the job for sure since we'd been campers there forever, but I hope they hire her too, because then summer will be perfect. I will miss my baby, Homer, though. Maybe he could be the camp mascot?

Now I'm wide awake and no one else in the house is.

THE GOOD
1. **Happiest:** When Homer came to live with me and when I fell in love with BB.
2. **Funniest:** In seventh grade when Emma accidentally walked into the boy's bathroom while talking to me.
3. **Sweetest:** When Dustin asked me to forgive him for the past.

THE BAD
1. **Saddest:** When MOM and DAD told me they were splitting up.
2. **Toughest:** When I knew I was going to have to turn BB in.
3. **Maddest:** When BB wrote me that stupid letter pretending I was some screwed-up girl who didn't matter to him.

THE DOWNRIGHT UGLY
1. **Grossest:** When Homer tipped over the trash bag, ate everything he could, and then threw up all over the kitchen floor. (Guess who cleaned up?)
2. **Scariest:** The time I was babysitting the twins last summer and they locked me out of their house (also qualifies as Stupidest).
3. **Wickedest:** Sleeping next to me every night.

Actually, I've been rethinking the whole WS thing. Granted, she is semi-evil by nature, but the other day at school I was walking to the car and heard her arguing with this uber prep Homecoming Queen:

"I think you're just jealous because my sister got so much attention! She should get a medal for being brave enough to turn that creep in!" said someone with a voice identical to WS's. I got closer and saw it <u>was</u> WS, which almost made me drop over in the parking lot.

In that second, I realized that she might be a really good nurse who would stick up for her patients. Of course, two minutes later she threw her book bag at me and told me I owed her big time for creating so many problems for her at school.

<u>W3TP: Relationships—who can figure any of them out?</u>
Posted 3/15 at 1:06 AM

o URock o ITalk

Wednesday, March 16

The most amazing thing has happened: a journalist from *Teen People* called and asked if she could interview me because she's writing an article about teen violence and how kids need to monitor each other. She actually read my story about BB (or part of it) on this blog! MOM and DAD said they weren't sure I should talk to her, but then WS convinced them it would be good for other kids to hear about it. (What alien has possessed Lola's body?)

After much negotiation, I talked to the reporter (MOM listened in), who sounded like she wasn't much older than me, and the questions she asked really made me think about everything that has happened this last year:

My parents getting divorced

Starting a new school

Finding love—losing love

Finding, having, losing, and then having trust again in a best friend

Being in therapy and taking antidepressants

The reporter didn't really care about all that stuff, though—I think she wanted me to say some really bad things about BB, but I just told her about how hard it was to make the decision to tell. She even asked for a picture of me, which was too cool because I happen to have an aunt who's a phenomenal photographer. That led to a photo-shoot party with Jules, Emma, Dustin, and me at the park!

W3TP: Trying to tell a serious story to someone but getting the feeling they already know what they want to say about you.
Posted 3/16 at 8:47 PM

20 URock 1 ITalk

wow we r going 2 b way famous grl! i can't wait 2 read all about it—which pic do u think they'll use?
Posted 3/16 at 8:55 PM by nujules4u

Friday, March 18

After what happened with BB, I decided I want to be like Aunt Sara and focus solely on my career. But then there was that lockdown, and now I've been doing a lot of thinking about Dustin. <u>What is wrong with me?</u> I tried to get some advice from Dr. White, but he just asked me the same question back as always:

"What do you think is wrong with you, Sadie?" This is said with the scientist-looking-through-a-microscope expression he likes to use.

To top it all off, I think MOM is getting serious about Charlie, who is way too old for her. He looks like he goes to a salon or something—his hair is too perfect (could it be a wig?), and WS told me she thinks he gets manicures too.

Aunt Sara told me (in confidence) that she thinks MOM and DAD are both going through some kind of *midlife crisis* where DAD tries to find a sweet young thing to make him feel like he's twenty again (eew) as MOM searches for the father figure she lost (their dad died when she was really little). She asked if any of my friends had parents who were going through a midlife crisis, and I had to say no. Jules has no parents to speak of, Dustin's mom is remarried and really happy, and Emma has a *normal* family.

<u>W3TP: A DAD dating a little girl, a MOM dating a grandpa, and an aunt dating no one.</u>
Posted 3/18 at 11:09 PM

6 URock o ITalk

Sunday, March 20

Dustin can drive now! He and Emma came over this afternoon, which made me infinitely thankful, because Charlie and MOM decided to go to brunch after mass, and that's too much Charlie for me. We rented a movie and hung out, and I thought about how weird it was that we might have been doing the exact same thing last year at this time.

Then, if life hasn't given me enough challenges, while my friends were there, DAD called and told me that he and Mabel broke up. He wanted me to feel all sorry for him, but I just couldn't. If my true self had spoken, I would have told him that I knew from the beginning she was way too young and spacey for him, but instead I said, "Daddy, come home. I still love you very much."

I'm not sure it helped because he sounded sadder and sadder. Then he asked a zillion questions about MOM and Charlie—I'm not even sure how he found out about the two of them—but I pretended Homer needed to go outside RIGHT AWAY. (Homer obliged by barking like crazy because I was waving around his squeaky toy, which he knows means playtime.)

When I hung up I felt really bad and mad and sad all at the same time, and that made me grouchy toward Dustin and Emma. They left pretty quickly after that. I couldn't help it. Mabel totally ruined our family and then dumped my DAD anyway. How messed up is that?

W3TP: Parents who try and make their kids feel sorry for something that's their own fault.
Posted 3/20 at 8:09 PM

10 URock 1 ITalk

Sades, that is 2 bad about ur dad but like Pastor Ken said in church, when we feel down, we must look up.
Posted 3/20 at 8:30 PM by sk8r4life

Sunday, March 27

I can't believe it! Aunt Sara called long distance and asked me if I would like to go on a trip with her during spring break as my birthday present. She just got a job assignment in NYC and thought maybe I could hang out with her there. It will be just the two of us for <u>three whole days</u>, and we can get room service and see a show and go shopping and walk around, which will be enough for me because both she and Jules told me every weird person on the planet seems to find a place to fit in there.

<u>W3TP: Being as insanely happy as I was depressed.</u>
Posted 3/27 at 6:03 PM

4 URock 1 ITalk

Don't 4get u promised 2 get 2gether with me over break!!!!!!!!!!!
Posted 3/27 at 11:23 PM by sk8r4life

Monday, March 28

Today's big (and unbelievable) news: WS got a full scholarship to nursing school! She says she is going to *transition* into a more nurselike appearance, and to start, she took out the two rings in her eyebrow. Can you believe it? Her scholarship includes the summer program, so she'll be out of here as soon as she graduates.

W3TP: The careers some people pick, like WS and Dr. White, and Mr. Hammacker, who looks like he bit into a lemon every day of school.
Posted 3/28 at 4:08 PM

6 URock 1 ITalk

U r so rite, i am taking vitamins now so i will never have ur sis as my nurse. cya!
Posted 3/28 at 4:15 PM by nujules4u

Tuesday, March 29

It totally sucks to have your birthday on a school day, but it totally rocks to finally get your very own cell phone. . . . At last I join the legions of other teens who can stay in touch anytime, anywhere. I also got a gift card that will get me at least one new outfit and a car key from WS, meaning . . . soon I can drive! I am starting to love my life!

W3TP: Not applicable on birthdays!
Posted 3/29 at 9 PM

10 URock 0 ITalk

Chapter Twenty

Monday, April 18

I'm in school, bored out of my skull, and suddenly remembered I haven't posted in ages. Here's everything I've been doing:

1. Going to NYC with Aunt Sara. It was unbelievable! She took me along on her photo shoot, which really made me realize that there is life after high school. I mean, look at how lucky she is now even without a guy in her life.

2. Hanging out with Dustin, who is still skateboarding but also driving a beat-up old Geo his parents got him for his birthday (which happens to be the day after mine). He and Emma come to my house all the time and we cruise around. We aren't boyfriend and girlfriend again, but we are pretty close, and I agreed to come to some of his competitions, since he still seems to think I help him do well. He says things are getting better for me because he prays for me every day, which is sort of sweet.

3. Working on the school newspaper: When I told Ms. Gardner about the *Teen People* reporter, she said it was the launch of my literary career and that I should keep a notebook of all the articles by or about me. She wants me to write something for the paper for next month and then be *on staff* until the school year ends. So I've been busting butt to keep my grades up and think of some interesting articles—how do reporters do it?

4. Now that a lot of time has gone by, Jules and me are truly back to being VBFs. She and Mona and Abby have come over for dinner on a few non-Charlie nights, so even our families are friends. Here's Jules's latest drawing of the two of us:

5. MOM and DAD let me switch to another therapist who is a social worker like MOM. Dr. White still orders my medicine, but Cat is the person I meet with every other week, and she sort of reminds me of Ms. Armstrong. She has a welcoming look on her face when I come into her office and never seems to get upset or bored with all the stuff I say.

W3TP: Not too much. I'm worried!
Posted 4/18 at 2:03 PM

o URock o ITalk

Saturday, April 30

Wow, I just read my last entry and can't even remember how I was feeling when I wrote it because so much has changed again. That seems to be the theme of my life this year, or perhaps it's just *part of the package a teenager gets,* as Cat says about a lot of things I tell her.

The incredible news is that DAD is moving back to Pennsylvania. I can hardly believe it! I still get sad sometimes that he and MOM aren't together (and they have said o&o that this is not a sign that they will), but at least he and I can eat Frooty Loops together on the weekends sometimes.

The other big news is that the *Teen People* article came out, and although there ended up being only two paragraphs about me and no picture, it was still pretty cool because this is what she wrote:

> "For a PA teen, tough love took on a
> new meaning when her boyfriend showed

her a gun he had stolen from his father, a police officer. Things got worse when 15-year-old Sadie Matthews suspected her boyfriend would bring the weapon to school and harm someone. Torn between her feelings and her fears, she says: 'It wasn't easy to turn him in, but in the end I knew I had to do it.'

It turned out that the Glock pistol was loaded and in her boyfriend's locker, so this courageous young woman may have saved many lives with her simple act of truth. Principal Turner says, 'I hope more students will follow Sadie's example and monitor their peers.'"

It was a little disappointing that it was so short—I talked to the reporter for at least an hour, but she emailed and told me her editor really cut down on her space and that she was sorry she couldn't write more.

"Sadie, you are truly fascinating," was the way she ended our conversation. No one has ever called me fascinating—how cool is that?

After I got involved in the school newspaper, I came up with the idea of Jules doing a cartoon for each issue, and Ms. G loved it. We call it "The Big Adventures of Blog Baby," and everyone seems to look forward to reading it on Fridays. Jules and I may have finally found our niche at school.

DAD is here every weekend now. He's wrapping up some things in St. Louis, but soon he'll be moving back for good.

W3TP: Still nothing. Maybe those pills really are magic. . . .
Posted 4/30 at 2:33 PM

4 URock o ITalk

Monday, June 6

This will probably be my last post for a while because I'm packing up for the summer. As soon as finals end, I'm off to be a camp counselor—yes, yours truly will be guarding a cabin of 11-year-olds, and it will probably make me wish it was last year when I had only twins to worry about. (Emma and Dustin got 7-year-olds, who are way easier to deal with.)

Cat thinks I will do fine without her this summer. She said I should email her a letter every week with updates, and keep up my blog if I can. (Cat has never been to Camp Winetaka, where the one computer in the place has a dial-up modem and is under lock and key.) I guess I can write her snail mail, though. I can't imagine Cat reading a chronicle of my life when she doesn't really have to, but then again, I never thought a reporter would read my site, either.

Jules is going to be a counselor with us too! Ms. Gardner wrote on Jules's reference that she was a gifted artist, so Jules is the *Assistant Activity Director,* which means she'll be stocking up on ideas for arts and crafts with popsicle sticks. She, Emma, me, and Dustin are going to start our own e-zine in the fall, with writing and poetry and art and lots of advice on starting a new high school—from firsthand experience, of course. (We've *agreed* the skateboarding content will be limited.)

Jules drew the <u>cutest</u> picture of us all ready for camp:

Now that she's leaving for the early-admit summer school, Lola has started to get all emotional about being my older sister, which is almost worse than her usual evil self. She even looks different—she took the purple dye out of her hair so it's ordinary brown, and no more nose ring. Where is the flaming goth I knew and hated? She's going to need a new life motto, and now I guess I'll have to switch to calling her BS. (I'll defer on the meaning until the end of summer.)

Slap is going to a school in California, a natural for him, so they won't see each other much, and Lola is superemotional about leaving him. As soon as Camp Winetaka is over, he's going to drive up to visit her and take me along for an end-of-summer shebang—how much fun will that be?

This year has been what Aunt Sara calls an "all's well that ends well" story, because Jules and me survived in spite of the challenges we faced. I'm still VBF with Emma, and who knows what will happen with Dustin? As for BB—maybe he really has repented and will make a new start of things in the military.

So I guess you could say I'm no longer a new girl. Next fall a new group will take my place, feeling all freaked out about their first day of school and wondering what the kids are like and whether there's any hope of a good life in the months ahead. Me and Jules have already decided what we need to do.

On the first day of school, we're going to request to be in the cafeteria for all three lunch periods. (I think Ms. Turner will say okay because I wrote a nice article about her in the school paper.) We'll stake out a table right at the exit of the lunch line and watch for all those kids with the nervous smiles and the desperate "where will I sit?" looks on their faces—just like the ones we had last year. That's when me and Jules will stand up and give them a big smile. There is no way they'll miss our sign—**New Kids Welcome Here**—or the seats we saved at our table, especially for them.

Posted 6/6 at 6:45 PM